## Only one of them was walking away from this confrontation alive

The pain from the wound in his arm was starting to burn fiercely, but the Executioner had suffered far worse in his time. He needed to finish Ms. Orange off.

Deciding it might be worth the risk, Bolan reached under his jacket for the SIG-Sauer.

As he did so, another lightning-fast crescent kick caught him on the side of his head. Ms. Orange followed it with a punch to the face that sent him stumbling backward.

But Bolan still had his hand on the SIG-Sauer. Stumbling back even farther than the punch had sent him, he got just enough distance so he could whip out the handgun and squeeze the trigger.

One bullet ripped through Ms. Orange's turtleneck and splintered her rib cage. Another followed it through the shattered bone and into her heart. As her eyes widened in shock, Ms. Orange collapsed to the ground.

She was good but the Executioner was better.

# MACK BOLAN ®
## The Executioner

# The Executioner

### Don Pendleton's®

# CODE OF HONOR

A GOLD EAGLE BOOK FROM

# W✺RLDWIDE®

TORONTO • NEW YORK • LONDON
AMSTERDAM • PARIS • SYDNEY • HAMBURG
STOCKHOLM • ATHENS • TOKYO • MILAN
MADRID • WARSAW • BUDAPEST • AUCKLAND

Recycling programs
for this product may
not exist in your area.

First edition December 2009

ISBN-13: 978-0-373-64373-8

Special thanks and acknowledgment to
Keith A. R. DeCandido for his contribution to this work.

CODE OF HONOR

**Printed in U.S.A.**

If Honour calls, where'er She points the way,
The Sons of Honour follow, and obey.

—Charles Churchill
1731–1764
*The Farewell*

When men of honor are disrespected, it is my duty to
avenge that wrong—whatever it takes. It is my code.

—Mack Bolan

# THE
# MACK BOLAN

## LEGEND

Nothing less than a war could have fashioned the destiny of the man called Mack Bolan. Bolan earned the Executioner title in the jungle hell of Vietnam.

But this soldier also wore another name—Sergeant Mercy. He was so tagged because of the compassion he showed to wounded comrades-in-arms and Vietnamese civilians.

Mack Bolan's second tour of duty ended prematurely when he was given emergency leave to return home and bury his family, victims of the Mob. Then he declared a one-man war against the Mafia.

He confronted the Families head-on from coast to coast, and soon a hope of victory began to appear. But Bolan had broken society's every rule. That same society started gunning for this elusive warrior—to no avail.

So Bolan was offered amnesty to work within the system against terrorism. This time, as an employee of Uncle Sam, Bolan became Colonel John Phoenix. With a command center at Stony Man Farm in Virginia, he and his new allies—Able Team and Phoenix Force—waged relentless war on a new adversary: the KGB.

But when his one true love, April Rose, died at the hands of the Soviet terror machine, Bolan severed all ties with Establishment authority.

Now, after a lengthy lone-wolf struggle and much soul-searching, the Executioner has agreed to enter an "arm's-length" alliance with his government once more, reserving the right to pursue personal missions in his Everlasting War.

# Prologue

Albert Bethke missed the cold war.

It was easier in those days. You had the United States, you had the Soviet Union, and you knew who the good guys were and who the bad guys were.

After the Berlin Wall came down, it all went to hell, as far as Bethke was concerned. Suddenly, they were working *with* the Soviets—or rather, the Russians, since there weren't Soviets anymore. Bethke supposed that was how the old OSS boys felt after World War II, when they brought over Nazi scientists to help with the cold war. But this particular new world order just didn't sit well with Bethke.

Still, he hung on with his job at the National Security Agency after twenty years in the FBI, and then had helped put the Department of Homeland Security together. But once DHS was up and running, he put in his retirement papers. He'd had enough.

Not that retirement was what he'd been expecting. At first, he did all the things he promised himself he'd get around to some day. He traveled all over the country, visiting the landmarks that he'd seen pictures and films of but never been to: the Grand Canyon, Mount Rushmore, the Empire State Building, the Statue of Liberty, the Southernmost Point of the U.S., and much more.

That took up three years, and then he was bored. Bethke had been both an administrator and a field agent, and he found he missed the excitement. Not enough to actually go back to work—though he had been told repeatedly by the directors at DHS that they'd take him back in a heartbeat—but enough to want to find more exciting things to occupy his time than play tourist.

So he found himself in New Paltz, New York, hiking in the Mohonk woodlands. Eventually, he planned to work his way up to proper mountain climbing, but hiking would do for now, help him rebuild his stamina. It would also get rid of the paunch that was developing. That paunch had put in appearances before, and it was always a signal to Bethke to get back into fieldwork.

Then, after a year or two of getting shot at, he'd go back behind a desk.

But that was all behind him.

It was the perfect day for a hike. It was a weekday, and it was drizzling, which meant that there was almost nobody else on the hiking trails. The few people he did see were doing the easier trails—Bethke went through the trees and up and down rocks.

The rain made it a bit more challenging, which made it that much more fun.

Bethke was dressed in brown hiking boots, white tube socks, a New York Mets baseball cap—which kept his thinning brown hair dry—cargo shorts and a plain white T-shirt, with a beige molle vest over it. Both the vest and shorts had plenty of pouches and big pockets, saving Bethke from having to bring a backpack. He carried bottles of water, power bars, his cell phone and .38 caliber bullets.

Those last were for the Smith & Wesson .38 Special in the shoulder holster that occasionally bit into his armpit as he climbed rocks or maneuvered around trees. The kids in both NSA and DHS had made fun of his "old-time" weapon. To Bethke, though, there was no point in a useless upgrade. Sure, he could go with a SIG-Sauer or a Glock or whatever the hell else they were using now, but as far as Bethke was concerned, a bullet was a bullet, and if you placed it right, it would do what you wanted it to do, regardless of what you shot it from.

In thirty years on the job, he'd never once missed what he was aiming at.

The kids would still razz him, of course, so Bethke would invite them down to the shooting range. Whoever grouped his or her shots closest would not have to pay for beer at the bar after they were off the clock. He'd even be generous and let them shoot first. They might do a decent job of grouping their shots in the chest or the head. Then Bethke would load his .38 Special and throw all six shots into the target in a perfect circle less than an inch in diameter.

Bethke never once paid for his own drink on those occasions.

He squeezed himself into a small passageway between two rocks, hoping there weren't any bears. He really didn't want to be in a position to have to shoot an innocent animal.

Once he made it through to the other side, he saw that a wooden ladder had been provided to get to the top of the rock. That was the end of this part of the hike, bringing him to a plateau that provided a great view of the area.

At the top was a no-longer-functional lighthouse, a few picnic tables, a public bathroom in a small stone structure, a very large rock that was sitting in the middle of the grass and mud and a spectacular view of Lake Mohonk. The mist from the clouds and rain covered the mountain like a blanket.

Best of all, Bethke didn't have to share it with anyone except for the young couple walking toward the lighthouse. He wished he'd had the foresight to bring a camera. His cell phone had one, but the quality was crap.

For a few seconds, he just stood and took in the view. Something was bothering him, though—he couldn't quite put his finger on it.

Then he very slowly turned his head so he was once again facing the couple, making it look as if he was simply gazing over the misty vista ahead of him.

The man was tall and skinny with short curly brown hair and plastic-rimmed glasses. He wore a loose-fitting rain slicker, denim shorts and hiking boots. His girlfriend or wife or whatever was very short and curvy, with wavy brown hair tied back into a ponytail, and was wearing a tight T-shirt that barely contained her large breasts. The shirt was untucked, hanging over a pair of what appeared to be elastic waistband sweat pants. She also wore hiking boots that seemed too big for her feet.

It could've been nothing. The man's slicker and woman's boots could simply have been too big. That sort of thing happened.

But the former could also be used to hide a holster and the latter to hide a knife sheath.

Then the man leaned in to whisper something in the woman's ear. She giggled, and he was smiling as he spoke, but when he leaned over, Bethke saw the outline of a bulge pressing against the slicker.

Bethke immediately dived to the ground and unholstered his .38. If he was overreacting, he'd apologize to the couple, but better safe than sorry. He'd made his share of enemies over the years, after all, and he couldn't risk that one of them might be here.

Even as he fell to the wet grass and mud, the man pulled out a 9 mm OD Green Glock 19, a compact model designed for carrying concealed.

It all happened fast enough that the man hadn't consciously registered that Bethke had dived to the ground, so his first shot went over his target's head.

Bethke needed a second to catch his breath—he'd just been doing a heavy hike, and his fatigued muscles and overtaxed lungs were reminding him just how long it had been since he'd done any kind of field work—and then he loosed a shot at the man.

As always, Bethke hit what he was aiming at: the man's center mass. The .38-caliber bullet sliced through the man's jacket and shirt like a hot knife through butter, cutting into his chest, splintering his ribs, and ripping into his heart.

The man squeezed off one more shot before he expired. A 9 mm round flew through the air and slammed into Bethke's left shoulder. He winced briefly against the pain of the bullet, which was now lodged in his rotator cuff—it wasn't the first time he'd been shot.

The woman had lifted her shirt, exposing a Charter Police Undercover .38 that was tucked into the waistband of her sweats, drew the weapon and fired off two shots that flew over Bethke's head.

That was just cover fire. She was diving behind her "husband's" corpse, using the body as a shield. That told him a lot about the level of ruthlessness Bethke was dealing with.

Knowing it was going to hurt like hell, Bethke rolled on the ground to take cover behind the rock. The woman's .38 rounds hit the mud where he'd been with a squelch, and others hit his Mets cap, which had fallen off while he rolled. More shots followed him until he was behind the protection of the rock.

Bethke took a moment to compose himself, even as the woman's last two rounds ricocheted off the rock.

"Hey!"

The voice came from behind Bethke. Whirling, with his back now to the rock, he saw an overweight man wearing a sweatshirt with the words Lake Mohonk emblazoned on the chest and white shorts running clumsily toward the tableau. He wore a backpack, and his ample belly was bouncing in rhythm with his strides.

"Hey, lady, what the hell're you doin'?"

His FBI instincts taking over, Bethke said, "Sir, get down!"

"That lady's nuts!" the fat man said, still running toward Bethke.

Then Bethke's spook instincts kicked in. The woman was an assassin who used her partner's body as a shield— yet this man was in her sights and she didn't shoot.

Which meant the fat man was part of the team. Bethke raised the S&W with his right hand and threw a shot. This was another reason why Bethke preferred his old-fashioned revolver: he could fire it with one hand, especially if he was leaning against a rock that could absorb the recoil.

The shot wasn't quite as perfect—it only hit the fat man in the shoulder, about an inch above his heart. It stopped him running, but even as blood stained his gray sweatshirt, he held up his left hand, which was holding a Hibben UC-458 throwing knife, which flew from his hand and lodged in Bethke's right thigh, cutting through skin and muscle and penetrating the femoral artery.

Feeling the blood start to pour out of his leg, Bethke squeezed off a second shot at the fat man. This one nailed him right between the eyes, splintering his skull and spattering blood all over the grass.

The fat man fell backward to the ground with a wet impact that kicked up quite a bit of mud. Bethke forced his left hand to clamp down on his right leg in what was probably a vain attempt to stanch the bleeding. The bullet wound in his shoulder wouldn't let him raise his left arm, but as long as he was seated on the ground, it was easy enough to try to hold the wound together. He also kept the knife in, since that was actually doing more than his hand was to keep the femoral artery from leaking out all over Mohonk Mountain.

It also meant he couldn't really move from this spot. The woman had had enough time while Bethke was dealing with the fat man to do any number of things, including possibly reload her .38.

Then the woman appeared before him. The muzzle of her erstwhile partner's Glock was staring Bethke right in the face. This close, Bethke could see the way she had modified her boots in order to hold knife sheaths. But she wouldn't even need those knives. Bethke toyed with the notion of raising his S&W, but she'd blow his head off before he could even start moving his arm.

Since he was pretty obviously dead anyhow, he tried to at least find out one thing. "Why?"

The woman shrugged, her ponytail bouncing. Bethke realized that he wouldn't get an answer. She and her two dead partners were probably hired assassins who were given a target. Such people were almost never told the why, only the who. If they were caught, they couldn't give any specifics to law enforcement.

Not that that was likely to be an issue for Bethke. He'd really hoped to climb Mount Kilimanjaro some day.

**1**

Mack Bolan peered through the Pentax Lightseeker XL scope on his ArmaLite AR-50 .50 BMG rifle. The scope was equipped with a Twilight Plex reticle that was designed for fast target acquisition and low light. It was currently in night-vision mode, not to adjust for darkness—since it was midafternoon—but to detect heat signatures on the other side of the steel plating of the warehouse.

To the general public, the warehouse in this suburb of Detroit, Michigan, was used for meat storage by the Hash & Cox Meat Packing Company. The inside was kept at thirty-eight degrees, so the presence of a ninety-eight-degree human being would stand out like a beacon in the scope.

At the moment, the warehouse was empty of everything other than the meat and assorted tools and storage units.

The Executioner knew that would change soon.

The warehouse wasn't exactly a front—Hash & Cox was a legitimate business that served as a middleman between suppliers and retailers—but it was used to mask a much less legitimate business. The warehouse was used for drug merchants who supplied cocaine and heroin for many of the dealers working in Detroit. All attempts by the Detroit Police Department to bring the business down had been stymied by Hash & Cox's CEO, Karl Hash—the brother-in-law of the DPD police chief. Attempts to bring in the DEA or the FBI were equally stymied by the influence of a state senator, who had received numerous campaign contributions from Hash & Cox and its satellite companies. Hash & Cox's COO, Charles McPherson, was also the nephew of a Michigan congressman who was on the committee that controlled the DEA's funding.

All this made Hash & Cox off-limits to legitimate law enforcement.

That was where the Executioner came in.

Bolan would bring the company down because nobody else could. He'd learned that McPherson and Hash were meeting at the warehouse to make sure that the place was cleaned out of all narcotics in preparation for an FDA inspection the following day. When Bolan had talked to a friend of a friend in the FDA to get the inspection to happen, he'd been hoping for this result. Hash and McPherson had too much riding on this warehouse to risk trusting underlings. They'd want to check the place themselves, make sure it would pass inspection.

He planned to take out the pair of them as soon as they showed up by taking up position on the roof of another warehouse on the same backstreet. With the pair of them dead, the path would be cleared to legitimately bring down the drug operation.

A limousine pulled up to the warehouse gate. The driver hopped out and fumbled with a set of keys before inserting one into the padlock that secured the chain holding the gate shut. The padlock snapped open, and the driver pulled the chain out and tossed it aside. The gate slowly creaked open on its own, leaving the way clear for the limo to continue inside, once the driver got back inside.

Once the limo pulled up to the side entrance, the driver again hopped out, opening the door to let the other occupants out: two white men in pinstriped suits who matched the pictures of Hash and McPherson in Bolan's dossier. At first, the Executioner was concerned that the driver might go inside as well, but he got back into the car once he closed the back door behind the two men. The scope couldn't differentiate people inside the warehouse, just heat signatures, and the warehouse had no windows.

He could have taken them down outside, but it was better to wait for them to be inside, so that the driver would remain in the dark for as long as possible. The driver himself aided in this by turning on the limousine's sound system at a very loud volume.

The Executioner had been waiting on the roof for these two to show up for four hours. He could hold off another minute.

After they went inside, Bolan waited until he saw two heat signatures. First one entered his sights, and he squeezed off a round. The rifle had been in his hands so long, it was like an extension of his arms, and firing it barely required a conscious effort on Bolan's part.

The .50-caliber bullet easily penetrated the thick metal of the wall and blew off the head of either Hash or McPherson. The formerly upright heat signature fell into a crumpled mess on the floor.

It took only a second for Bolan to adjust his aim slightly and take out the heat signature of the second person, who hadn't yet registered what had happened to his colleague. The bullet whistled through the air and pulped the head of the target.

When the second body went down, Bolan continued his vigil, making sure the heat signatures didn't move and the driver didn't respond to the loud report of two rifle shots being fired. After a while, the signatures got cooler as their body temperatures went down, accelerated by the low temperatures inside the warehouse.

But Bolan still didn't move.

The limo sound system had been going for four songs before the driver turned it off. Seconds later, he bounded out of the car, a cell phone at his ear and a concerned look on his face, and ran to the entrance. Bolan assumed that Hash and McPherson had only expected to be a minute or two inside, and that the delay had the driver worried.

As well it should have.

Only then did the Executioner remove the scope and head for the roof entrance.

After making his way down the stairs of the warehouse to the street, he placed the rifle and scope in the trunk of the Chevrolet Aveo he'd rented, got behind the wheel and drove toward Interstate 94. Using his secure sat phone, he dialed the number for Stony Man Farm, the base for America's ultracovert counterterrorist organization.

Within seconds, he was put through to Hal Brognola.

"Both men have been taken care of," Bolan said without preamble, and without specifics.

"Good work, Striker. Your ride's waiting at the Selfridge Air National Guard Base to bring you back here. We've got a big one."

Bolan's original plan had been to drive south on I-94 to Detroit, where he'd hole up in a motel room for the night, but instead he headed to Selfridge.

A FALCON 10 PRIVATE JET belonging to Stony Man had been waiting for Bolan at Selfridge, and it took off shortly after his arrival. One of the airmen stationed at the base said he would take care of Bolan's rental car. The Executioner knew that Brognola had contacts all over the military and in law enforcement, and it was no surprise that he'd gotten Selfridge to do him this favor without their knowing precisely what it was about—or who it was they were doing it for.

The Falcon 10 had only one occupant when Bolan arrived: Charlie Mott, a civilian pilot who sometimes flew for Stony Man. "Welcome aboard, Striker," Mott said with a sloppy salute at Bolan's approach.

"Since when does Brognola give you chauffeur duty?" Bolan asked, as he climbed the small set of steps leading to the aircraft's interior.

As he pulled the steps up into the closed-door position behind Bolan, Mott said, "He wanted to make sure you got to the Farm in one piece. He said this one's a biggie."

"So he told me over the phone."

Mott then went into the cockpit and started preparing the plane for takeoff.

The Executioner slept for most of the two-hour flight to Stony Man Farm in the Blue Ridge Mountains of Virginia. The Falcon 10 could accommodate up to eight people in extremely comfortable seats, and Bolan had long ago learned to take his rest where he could get it.

Mott taking the Falcon 10 into its final descent was enough to awaken Bolan, and as soon as the plane touched down, he gathered his rifle case and satchel and waited for the aircraft to come to a stop.

Brognola was waiting for him on the runway of the Farm's airfield. "Welcome back, Striker. Let's head up to the farmhouse so you can get a shower and a change of clothes. I've got a full briefing ready to go as soon as you're ready."

"No need to wait. You obviously want to get going quickly on this."

"Fine." Brognola hadn't expected Bolan to actually accept any delay in getting the briefing to his next mission, but he had made the offer in any case out of respect for the man.

He and Bolan walked the short distance to the farmhouse, rather than accepting a ride in the Jeep that was standing by. After walking up the front steps and keying in the proper access code, the two men made their way to the War Room. A solid wooden conference table, surrounded by ergonomic chairs, dominated the room. At one end was a state-of-the-art laptop with a twenty-inch monitor. A USB cable was plugged into the laptop at one end and into a huge plasma TV mounted on the far wall, showing what was on the computer's monitor in high definition.

At the moment, that was the desktop, which had assorted icons of programs and folders with file names made of seemingly random alphanumeric characters. Bolan knew that these were codes. Brognola moved the cursor to one of those folders and double-tapped the laptop's track pad.

The folder contained several Portable Network Graphics files, also given coded alphanumeric file names.

First, Brognola called up four of the images, which were all crime-scene photos of dead bodies, and arranged them on the screen so Bolan could see all four.

There was a man with thinning brown hair lying against a rock in a grassy area, a woman with short steel-gray hair lying dead in a city street with a bullet wound in her back, an overweight man with his head literally blown off in a parking lot and a bald man with multiple stab wounds in his chest.

"You're looking at Albert Bethke, Michaela Grosso, Terrence Redmond and Richard Lang."

Bolan started at the third name. "Redmond's been retired from the NSA for, what, ten years?"

"Twelve. And that's something he has in common with the other three. They're all people with a history of covert ops, and they're all retired. Bethke was one of the people who set up DHS after 9/11, and before that he was NSA and FBI. Grosso and Lang were both CIA. They were all killed over the course of the past week or so—assassinated by the Black Cross."

"You're sure?"

Brognola hesitated. "No. But the evidence points to it."

"The lack of evidence, you mean."

"Yes," Brognola said reluctantly. "There's virtually no evidence at any of the crime scenes. No hairs, no fibers, no fingerprints save those of the victims, no biological residue for DNA save those of the victims, no shell casings or bullets at the scene or in any of the bodies despite the presence of bullet wounds, and almost all the blood traces that aren't compromised by liberal application of bleach are also the victims'." Brognola called up several more files, which were also digital photos. "Any number of killings over the years have matched this total lack of evidence. The FBI has a file a mile long on these—I know, 'cause I'm the one who started it. Of course, some of those are your executions, but the ones that aren't…"

"The rumors about the Black Cross go back to my Army days," Bolan said. "An elite group of assassins made up of the best of the best."

"I know. And I know that there's nothing to support it." He sighed. "Unfortunately, just because the theory fits the evidence—or lack of same—doesn't mean it's right. And we've got nothing solid, except for the fact that local police were completely stymied. They kicked it up to FBI, and they brought it to me."

Bolan scratched his chin thoughtfully. "When you referred to the evidence, you said 'virtually' and 'almost.' What's different about these crime scenes from all the other ones you think are Black Cross?"

Brognola actually smiled at that, pleased that Bolan noticed how carefully he'd chosen his words. "Not 'these,' just the one. Bethke was killed in the Mohonk woodlands in New York. Two distinct sets of blood evidence were bleached far away from Bethke's body— but there were a few drops of blood that *weren't* bleached, *and* didn't belong to Bethke. DNA identifies it as belonging to a former sharpshooter in Baltimore City PD's Quick Response Team named Bert Hanson. He retired after only nine years on the job and then fell off the grid."

"You think Black Cross recruited him?" Bolan asked.

"Makes sense. If I was looking for assassins, the QRT would be on my list of possible recruiting sources. Hanson had been a model cop—several decorations, no bad notes in his jacket. And then, out of nowhere, he quits, no reason given, and he's not been heard from since—until he bled on the ground at Mohonk."

"So what does that get us?"

In response, Brognola double-tapped another graphics file, which called up the face of a walleyed man with a thick beard, a large nose and curly hair. "I did a little digging into Hanson's departure from the BPD. This is somebody who met with him at BPD's Western District headquarters shortly before he quit. They talked in an interrogation room. He signed in as a lawyer, so there's no audio of their meeting, but the name he signed in with doesn't match any lawyer in the Maryland State Bar Association. So I ran his face through the database and eventually got a hit."

Double-tapping on yet another file brought up another picture of the same man, but with the beard shaved off and thick-lensed glasses over the walleyes. "The only name we have for him is Galloway, and he's been seen with a wide variety of dodgy personalities. Terrorists, arms dealers, assassins, you name it. But nobody's ever been able to pin anything on him, or even find out his first name."

"You think he's recruiting for the Black Cross?"

Nodding, Brognola said, "Yes. And he's a regular attendee of the Valley Forge Gun Show. He doesn't have a booth, he just attends as a citizen. That show runs three or four times a year, and one of them is this weekend."

"Hence your rush?"

"Yes. You think the Black Cross would be interested in gaining a new member?"

Bolan took a sip of his coffee. "Only one way to find out."

"Good. We've already created a new identity for you."

Raising an eyebrow, the Executioner asked, "Why not simply use the Matt Cooper ID?"

"He fits the profile, but this op risks burning that ID completely, and it's too useful." Brognola minimized all the files so the desktop was revealed once again, and this time he double-tapped another folder.

Several files became visible in the window, and Brognola called up several of them. One had a recent picture of Bolan, with a caption that read Michael Burns. Another had a U.S. Marines dossier that revealed Burns was a rifleman who served in the first Gulf War, but was dishonorably discharged due to insubordination—specifically for killing a prisoner after being told to bring him in alive.

"I see Bear's been busy," Bolan said, referring to Aaron "the Bear" Kurtzman, Stony Man's computer expert.

"I had a feeling you were going to say yes to this one, Striker."

"I know how important the Black Cross is to you, Hal."

Brognola waved him off. "I don't care about that— I just want these people stopped."

"Redmond and the others served their country with honor and deserved a quiet retirement. I will take down whoever killed them."

Nodding, Brognola said, "Well, Michael Burns should be a good fit for them. He's got the skills, and he was kicked out of the Marines for killing someone. He's been working as a mercenary for a few years, but he's had trouble finding work because he uses excessive force regardless of the circumstances."

"Just what a group that deals only in excessive force would be looking for."

"And Bear's made sure that any background check will come up solid. Only one of his old COs in the Corps is still alive, and he's a friend of mine, so he'll vouch for 'Burns.'"

Peering at the screen, Bolan said, "He's from Alabama?"

"Yes. Tomorrow's the last day of the gun show, so you can get a good night's sleep, and you can head up to King of Prussia in the morning."

The Executioner stood up, shook Brognola's hand, then headed out of the meeting room to get that shower the head of Stony Man had offered.

While Bolan was still skeptical of the existence of the Black Cross, he also knew that, if they *did* exist, they needed to be shut down. For them to have been successful for so long spoke to an organization that was responsible for murder on a truly massive scale.

Bolan intended to make sure they would be stopped once and for all.

2

After a four-hour drive up I-81 and across I-76 in a specially modified Ford Escort owned by Stony Man, the Executioner arrived in King of Prussia, Pennsylvania, and the Valley Forge Convention Center for the last day of the Valley Forge Gun Show. The convention exhibit hall was filled with booths run by sports shops, gun stores, and dealers who sold weaponry and assorted accessories.

Before entering, Bolan was frisked and put through a metal detector. The gun show had very specific regulations: all firearms had to be checked and rendered inoperable and no loaded firearms were permitted inside the convention center during the open hours of the show. Rather than ever be forced to relinquish any of his weaponry, Bolan chose to do so voluntarily by simply leaving everything in the car. It was a strange feeling walking around without weapons on his person, but he took solace in the fact that he wasn't alone in that.

After paying his nine-dollar admission fee, Bolan walked the floor, inspecting some of the firearms, knives and accessories. There was nothing here he wasn't already intimately familiar with, especially since he often had access to weaponry that wasn't yet ready for the open market. Still, he pretended to be interested as men in ballcaps enthusiastically waxed rhapsodic on the subject of their particular items and why they were better than those of the guy across the hall.

Bolan played along, asking the types of questions that a civilian might ask, and he noted at least three occasions where the booth jockey in question exaggerated the ability of the weapon he was trying to sell.

He found himself spending some time at one booth, where an old man with a thick white beard was selling an impressive collection of knives. "This," the man said in a scratchy voice, "is what you really want, my friend."

The old man slid the glass off a wooden case and tilted it upward. Reaching around, he grabbed a black-colored folding knife. The blade itself was also obsidian in color, and had a stylized logo etched into the flat of the blade.

"This here's an Emerson Commander BTS," the old man said as he held it handle out to Bolan. "Down in Atlanta, they voted this best overall knife of the year."

Bolan knew of the honor bestowed by the International Blade Show, and also knew the answer to the question he posed as he took the knife from the dealer. "How's it different from the CQCs?"

"Oh, the CQCs're fine for your average use, but lookin' at you, I'm thinkin' you're more the combat-knife type."

"I thought the CQCs *were* combat knives."

"They are—but if you want the *best,* you want the Commander. Lasts longer, flips open faster and is just tougher. Sure, the CQCs are *good*—the Commander's *better.*"

The weight, Bolan noted, was good.

"Thank you," he said, handing the knife back to the man.

"Not interested, huh?" A smile peeked out from the old man's thick beard. He replaced the knife, set down the Emerson case and slid back the glass. Then he pointed at another one, containing Masters of Defense Beshara knives. "How 'bout these?"

Bolan let himself be lectured on the relative merits of the old man's knives, all the while taking glances around in search of Galloway. At one point, he put on a shame-faced tone, and said, "Sorry, I'm supposed to be meeting a friend here, and he's late. Can I see the XSF-1?"

Eventually, he thanked the old man and excused himself, continuing to walk the floor, but still no sign of Galloway after several hours.

Just then, the Executioner saw a short man with curly hair and walleyes heading toward a gun-shop booth. He was wearing a pair of thick-lensed glasses, though different from the set in the picture Bolan had seen at Stony Man. He had also grown back the beard, though it wasn't as full as it had been in the older picture, and had flecks of gray in it now. Galloway was wearing a denim jacket that had seen better decades over a stained white T-shirt, and frayed blue jeans with a hole in the left knee and another in the rear left pocket.

From there, it was a simple tail operation. The convention hall was crowded enough that Bolan didn't have to worry much about Galloway noticing him. The booths were arranged in a grid pattern, so Bolan made as if he were simply working his way up and down the aisles. He took the opposite route Galloway took, so he would pass the target once in each aisle.

Galloway, Bolan noticed, didn't spend very much time looking at the guns, but instead seemed to be focused on the people. One would expect no less from a recruiter. He also tended to spend a lot of time staring at the few women who were attending. Some of the shops even had so-called "booth babes," scantily clad models hired to attract men to their merchandise. Galloway even tried chatting a couple of them up. But they all went to the default sales pitch and deflected any and all attempts at personal conversation with the ease of long practice.

Eventually, Galloway worked his way to the food court, at which point Bolan walked up to an ammunition dealer and pointed at a rifle bullet. Putting on a Southern accent, he asked, "That there a .50 caliber round? Looks a mite too small."

The dealer, a tall, wiry man with large brown eyes and whose hands never seemed to stop moving, said, "This, sir, is a .416 Barrett rifle round. This is the newest in rifle armament, know what I'm sayin'? This is *infinitely* superior to those crappy old .50 cals. That's old school, and with all due respect to old school, this is *new* school, know what I'm sayin'?"

"How's it better, exactly?" Bolan asked, already knowing the answer.

"This puppy shoots flatter and faster than the .50s, and also hits *way* harder, know what I'm sayin'?" The man flailed his arms a bit and then picked up a .50-caliber shell and held it next to the .416. "Now I know what you're thinking right now."

Bolan was fairly sure he didn't, but let him go on.

"You're thinking to yourself, 'How can a bullet that's

of a *lesser* caliber be better than a bullet of a *greater* caliber?' That there's the beauty of this here round, is that the shorter height allows for much greater speed and durability."

Having satisfied himself that enough time had passed, the Executioner said, "Good to know. Thankee kindly, mister. I'll definitely be considerin' this next time I'm buyin' me some huntin' rounds."

"Good man." The dealer put down the shells and flailed a few more times. "You sure I can't convince you to purchase a few now?"

"Nah, I'm just grazin'." With that, the Executioner headed off to the food court in the hopes of finding precisely what he was looking for.

The food court was the typical sort for a convention center. An entire section of wall was taken up with a metal counter, behind which were limp-looking hot dogs, stale popcorn, limp, packaged salads, uninspiring packaged sandwiches, soggy pizza and fountain soda, all priced in excess of market value.

Because of that, the large round tables in front of the counter were sparsely occupied. Each table sat up to eight people comfortably, but none was fully occupied. One had a couple seated at it, enjoying each other's company more than the food. Another had three men, all wearing flannel shirts and ballcaps, discoursing loudly on the subject of the best hunting grounds in central Pennsylvania. Another was occupied by two couples who were discussing whether the Philadelphia Phillies had another shot at winning the division that year.

Galloway sat alone at another table, hungrily biting

into a slice of pepperoni pizza and washing it down with a large soda.

Not really trusting the food to do good things to his gastrointestinal tract, the Executioner limited himself to a diet cola from the fountain. Once he paid for it, Bolan walked casually to the table where Galloway sat chewing on his pizza, the grease from the pepperoni dripping into his beard and onto his T-shirt.

Still affecting the Southern accent, Bolan said, "Mind if I sit a spell, mister?"

Galloway shrugged. "It's a free country." He spoke in a raspy voice.

"Yeah, that's what they tell me, anyhow. You here buyin'?"

Mouth full of pizza, Galloway said, "Window-shopping."

"Right there with you, mister. See, I can't afford most of the firearms hereabouts. Hell, I can't even afford none of the food beyond this here pop. Good thing it's only nine bucks to get in."

"Things are tough all over," Galloway said, swallowing his pizza and grabbing his own soda.

"Don't I know it. Man with my skills I ought to be able to be drownin' in work, but the damn Marines had other notions."

"You served?"

"You betcha. Rifle company Baker two-niner. Was a gunnery sergeant, till they kicked me out, anyhow. Served in the Gulf the first time."

"Discharged?"

"Yup. And not the honorable kind, neither. Thought the notion was to kill the enemy, not coddle 'em." Bolan sipped his soda, then set it down and held out a hand. "Sorry, my momma raised me better than this. Name's Michael Burns."

Galloway accepted the handshake but did not return the introduction. "Pleased to meet you, Sergeant Burns."

Bolan noticed that Galloway's handshake was clammy and greasy, the latter no doubt from the pizza. "Been almost fifteen years since anybody called me that, mister. Just call me Michael."

Breaking the handshake, Galloway said, "You can call me Galloway. You looking for work, Michael?"

"Well, I'm gainfully employed, if that's whatcha mean, but it ain't nothin' that makes use of my skills, if you follow me. Still in uniform, but it's the type where they issue you a mop and bucket 'stead of a sidearm and holster. Been a few years since I got me that kinda work— *man's* work." He shook his head. "Goddamn Marines."

"Well, Michael, I might be able to help you out. You have a card?"

Bolan snorted. "You're kiddin', right? Kinda business I'm in—"

Galloway held up a hand. "Of course. How long are you in town?"

"Due back at my job tomorrow—'less, of course, I got me a reason to call in sick?"

"I'd say you do." Galloway reached into his denim jacket pocket and pulled out a small spiral notepad and a pen. He wrote something down and ripped the page out of the notepad. Handing it across the table, Galloway said, "Come to this address tomorrow at noon. Consider it a job interview."

Bolan hesitated, staying in character. "Job interview?

Hang on a sec, mister, we're just talkin' here. I mean, I was just lookin' for some conversation, if you follow me. I ain't trollin' for—"

"Maybe not, but if you're what you say you are, the people I represent might be interested in you—especially since we had a couple of job openings recently."

Drawing himself up, and still not taking the paper, Bolan said, "The hell you mean, what I say I am? You callin' me a liar, Galloway?" He also noted the line about job openings. If he really did represent Black Cross—or whoever killed those retired operatives—then it was likely that the bloodstains at Mohonk Mountain represented dead bodies, not just wounded ones. If so, the Executioner was impressed that Bethke had been able to take down one or two of his killers—though it was small comfort.

Holding up his hands, the paper flapping with the motion, Galloway said, "No, Michael, I'm not calling you a liar, not at all. But some soldiers have been known to exaggerate their accomplishments a bit."

Surprised that someone who worked with ex-military types would make such a blunder, confusing an Army soldier with a Marine, Bolan said, "Look, they may've discharged me, but I'm a *Marine*, not a soldier. We don't lie—we leave that to the soldiers an' sailors an' airedales."

"Fair enough," Galloway said quickly. "Look, let's just call this a fortuitous coincidence, all right?" He held out the paper again.

Bolan snatched it. It was stained with pepperoni grease, but it provided an address on North Gulph Road.

"That's in the park across the street," Galloway said. Nodding, Bolan said, "I know it, yeah." It was the

Valley Forge National Historical Park, which commemorated the famous Revolutionary War battle fought in this area in the winter of 1777–1778.

"Good. Maybe we can do business."

"Just came here for pleasure, Galloway—but hey, if business comes out of it, I ain't gonna complain."

Popping the last of his pizza into his mouth, Galloway said, "Sometimes things work out."

"Reckon they do, yeah." Bolan placed the slip of paper into his pocket. "Guess I'll see you tomorrow then, Galloway, huh?"

Galloway got to his feet, holding his cup of soda and gathering up the empty plate and paper napkin. "I hope so, Michael."

He went to the nearest garbage can and dumped the plate and napkin, then headed toward the restroom.

The Executioner finished his soda, dropped it into the same garbage can, then headed straight for the exit. He needed to find a place to stay for the night. The convention center had two hotels attached to it, and since this was the last day of the show, there were likely to be rooms available.

Next day, he would start his quest to see if the Black Cross was real. And if it was, it wouldn't be for much longer.

## 3

The woman who killed Albert Bethke sat by the pool in a Cayman Islands resort, watching the men watch her. She was wearing as skimpy a bikini as she could get away with, along with large sunglasses and a straw hat to protect her from the tropical sun. Bobby pins kept the hat secure on the red-haired wig she wore, as the trade winds occasionally blew through with particular force, funneled by the two thirteen-story towers of the resort hotel. The hat had a purple band with a large flower on the side. She kept her hotel room key inside that band.

The remnants of a margarita sat next to her. The bartender had put salt on the rim of the glass, despite her specifically requesting it without.

She'd enjoyed her vacation—salted margarita notwithstanding. It was also business related, as her bank account was down here, and she preferred to check on her money in person rather than online. There was something satisfying about checking it in person, being able to touch your own money, so to speak.

She was born in Russia with the name Ida Kaprov, but nobody had called her that name for six years. At the age of ten, she and her family emigrated to the U.S., living in suburban New Jersey. She attended UCLA and was recruited by the Los Angeles Police Department, which was trying to bust a crime ring that was using Eastern European immigrant women for online sex shows, prostitution, strip clubs and escorts—and also as drug mules.

The bust was a success, in large part due to her efforts. She'd proved herself a natural at undercover work, and had continued to work undercover, first for the LAPD, then for the FBI. Her ability to speak Russian combined with her stunning good looks and hourglass figure made her a valuable asset. Men in particular were susceptible to her charms.

In addition, she was a crack shot, having scored the highest rating of any woman in LAPD history on the shooting range. She'd even considered applying for the SWAT team, but her superiors convinced her that she was better off as an undercover agent.

Ida quickly grew disillusioned with law enforcement, however. The institutionalized sexism was stifling, and the very qualities that made her good undercover also made her a target for her Neanderthal colleagues. Plus, she found the restrictions to be far too binding. Most of the people arrested in her cases didn't deserve to wait for trial, they simply should have been shot between the eyes, ridding the Earth of their filth once and for all.

The straw that broke her back was seven years after she'd first been recruited. She found herself infiltrating another online sex-prostitution-stripper-escort ring that was run by the same people as the group she'd helped bring down as a new recruit—they'd never seen a day of jail time for the bust years earlier.

Sure enough, they got off *again,* and this time Ida followed up on some rumors she'd heard about a group of elite assassins called the Black Cross. The finest assassins in the world, they would kill anyone for a price and were never traced.

However, such quality did not come cheap. But by this time, her parents had died, leaving her with a sizable inheritance, which combined with her own life savings, allowed her to put a hit on the two men and one woman who ran the ring.

After they died, the Black Cross asked her if she wanted to join them.

On that day, Ida Kaprov died and "Ms. White" was born. The Black Cross's operatives were all given names based on color. The Black Cross had stayed operational over the years due to its tight security, including their members not being identifiable even to one another.

The last op had been particularly gratifying. The fact that she was the only survivor of a three-person team actually gave her a particular thrill. It made her feel that she was better than anyone else—certainly better than Mr. Green and Mr. Mauve, who'd both been killed by the target—and that was a compelling rush.

She decided that she deserved a reward.

Gazing around the pool, she tried to figure out which of the men drooling over her curvy figure, barely contained by the tiny fabric of her bikini, she would take back to her room.

She rejected three as too old, two as too tanned, and one as too young.

That left her with two choices: the dark-haired man in the purple Speedo with the lean, muscular body, or the blond-haired man in blue bathing trunks with the wide shoulders.

When a woman came over to the dark-haired man and kissed him, Ms. White realized that she had only one choice. Not that she didn't sometimes enjoy the challenge of seducing a man who was already attached, but she didn't feel like going to that level of effort this day.

After finishing off the remnants of her margarita, Ms. White got to her feet and walked slowly to the blond-haired man. He had been openly staring at her for quite some time, until he realized she was heading for him, at which point he made a show of staring at the pool, the bar, the hotel, the palm trees—anything *except* her.

She pushed her sunglasses down her nose so she could peer at him from over the frame. "You've been staring at me for over an hour now."

He looked around nervously, not making eye contact. "Um—"

"Are you denying it?" She spoke in a mildly harsh tone.

"I, uh—" Then he broke down, looked at her and smiled. "I guess I really can't, huh?" His voice was deep and pleasant, like waves crashing over rocks.

She smiled back. "Do you like what you see?"

"Wouldn't have been staring if I didn't. Nothin' in the world better than a curvy redhead, I always say."

"Do you want to see more?"

The smile widened, showing perfect white teeth. "Not much left to see."

"Oh, but it's worth it. You have a room here?"

Within minutes, they were in the hallway outside his room, and he was fumbling in the fanny pack he'd brought with him to the pool containing money, ID, and his room key. Eventually, he liberated the plastic card and inserted it into the slot. The green light came on, and he pushed the door open.

The moment the door closed behind her, she grabbed the blond-haired man by the back of his head, turned him around and started kissing him.

He returned the kiss hungrily, his tongue sliding into her mouth.

Conveniently, they were both wearing very little, so it was the work of only a second or two for him to remove her bikini and her to remove his swimming trunks. Her straw hat, however, remained on her head, still secured by the bobby pins, as did the wig.

They remained kissing while standing upright, now both naked, and peering between his legs, she could see how pleased he was by this turn of events. Eventually, she maneuvered him to one of the room's two double beds, throwing him playfully but forcefully onto his back.

She pleasured him for a minute or two, as she often did to make sure that the man she was with was fully aroused. That was often not much of a concern, but she knew that her partners enjoyed it. He also reached down and tried to fondle her breasts; she admired his enthusiasm.

Finally, she climbed onto the bed, her legs straddling his hips, and lowered herself onto him. They both moaned with the pleasure of the moment as she rocked her hips.

Within only a few seconds, though, she could feel his body tense as he started to climax.

Reaching up, she slid her hand under the brim of the straw hat and pulled out one of the Hibben throwing knives that she'd taken off the corpse of the late, unlamented Mr. Mauve.

Just as the blond man climaxed, moaning in pleasure, Ms. White plunged the point of the Hibben knife into his carotid artery.

Ms. White felt his death throes combined with his pleasure, and only then did she also climax, as blood gushed all over the hotel bed from the wound she'd created.

For several seconds, Ms. White sat there, feeling the pleasure crest over her.

Then she climbed off the corpse and yanked the knife from its neck. More blood poured out of the wound, though it no longer gushed, with the heart having stopped pumping.

Turning around and not giving the young man another thought, Ms. White went into the bathroom to wash off her right hand, which was the only place she'd gotten blood on herself. Over the years, she'd perfected this particular sequence of events to the point where she got no blood on her whatsoever—except on the hand that wielded the killing knife. She'd yet to figure out a way to entirely avoid that.

Leaving her hand wet rather than risk leaving any trace evidence on the hotel towel, Ms. White went back into the room, climbed into her bikini bottoms and tied the bikini top.

After she exited the hotel room, she headed to the crossover bridge to the other tower where her own room was, retrieving her key from the band in her hat. Once inside, she removed both hat and wig and tossed them into the bathtub. Pausing to remove the battery from the room's smoke detector, Ms. White then grabbed a book of matches from the hotel restaurant that she'd tossed on the desk the night before. She struck one match, lighting it, and set the hat and the wig on fire.

As both items burned, Ms. White removed the bikini bottoms, then the female condom, wrapping it in a bit of toilet paper. She'd dispose of it later, somewhere off the hotel grounds. She put a T-shirt over the bikini top, then donned a pair of panties and khaki shorts. Reaching into the shorts pocket, she opened her cell phone and discovered a text message that simply read: Call.

She dialed the current number for the Black Cross headquarters, which was in a cabin in the Redwood forests of Humboldt County, California—this month. A voice on the other side said, "Ms. White, return to base ASAP."

"I'll be on the next plane," she said. "I'm finished here anyhow."

AFTER CHECKING OUT of the resort, using the credit card of one of her many false identities, Ms. White booked a flight to the Eureka/Arcata Airport in Northern California using a different ID. There was a delay in the connecting flight at Bob Hope Airport in Burbank, but eventually she arrived safely.

As expected, the Black Hawk piloted by Mr. Silver was waiting to take her from Eureka/Arcata to Black Cross HQ. When the Black Hawk landed, she was met by the tall, dark-skinned, bald-headed Mr. Indigo. He stared at her with his wide, intense brown eyes, and said, "Welcome home."

Unlike most other heterosexual men, Mr. Indigo didn't stare at her chest, even though the flower-print sundress she had changed into showed considerable cleavage. For his part, Mr. Indigo was, as always, wearing an immaculate charcoal three-piece suit. Were it not so immaculate, Ms. White would have been convinced that he slept in it, since he never wore anything else in her presence.

As he accompanied her to the cabin that was a quarter mile from the airfield, Mr. Indigo said, "Our man Galloway found a potential new recruit. Given the way we've been hemorrhaging operatives lately…"

Ms. White nodded. Besides Misters Mauve and Green, another operative had been killed in the Redmond assassination, and three more had retired. They were down to only six, and she knew that Mr. Indigo preferred their fighting strength to be an even dozen.

"Who is this new man?"

They entered the cabin, and Mr. Indigo led her to a laptop, which had a generic screen saver running on the monitor. Mr. Indigo touched the button under the track pad, causing the screen to change to that of a U.S. Marine Corps dossier on a gunnery sergeant. His name was blacked out—a standard Black Cross security protocol.

"He's a former jarhead," Mr. Indigo explained, "and he's been a merc since then. Sharpshooter. He's had trouble finding work lately because he's too brutal."

"I wasn't aware that you *could* be too brutal for the Marines."

Giving her the tiniest of smiles—which was as emotional as he ever got—Mr. Indigo said, "There's a first time for everything. He has a tendency to kill people regardless of whether they're *supposed* to be killed, which irked his superiors in the Corps. After that, he became a merc, and that same tendency irked a few of his employers, too."

"I can imagine," Ms. White said. "We have no such compunctions, though."

"Indeed not. Galloway has him set up for his interview tomorrow. I want you to pick the talent for it and supervise the process."

Ms. White blinked. That was something usually left to operatives with more experience than her. "Why me?"

"I'd say you've earned the promotion." Mr. Indigo stared at her with those intense eyes. "You've been my best operative since you were hired six years ago. With Mr. Red, Mr. Brown and Ms. Violet retiring, and losing Mr. Green, Mr. Mauve and Ms. Yellow, you're the one I trust the most right now."

Unsure if she was being complimented, or if she was simply the best of a series of bad choices, Ms. White instead just asked, "Where is the interview to be held?"

"Valley Forge. Find a half dozen or so from the usual sources and get them set up at eleven tomorrow. The interview's at noon."

Ms. White winced. That was all the way across the country, which meant she'd need to leave immediately to have time to set things up.

However, Mr. Indigo wasn't one to give compliments lightly. If he was going to trust her with such an operation, it meant good things for her. Specifically, it meant more pay—which was, after all, her primary motivation—given his use of the word *promotion*. The idealistic college student who'd thought she'd be doing some good in the world had long since died. The realities of life beat that idealism right out of her.

Mr. Indigo opened another window on the laptop. "There's an e-ticket in the name of Alma White at

Eureka/Arcata for a flight to Denver, and then a connecting flight to Philadelphia. You've got one hour."

    Just enough time to shower and change her clothes. She
wanted to get the smell of the blond man off her anyhow.

**4**

Bolan drove the Ford Escort down North Gulph Road to the location on the greasy slip of paper given to him the previous day by Galloway. North Gulph was one of many roads that led through Valley Forge National Historical Park.

The Executioner thought it repugnant that someone like the Black Cross—if it was indeed behind all this—would sully the heroic sacrifice of the soldiers who fought against tyranny on this ground in the eighteenth century with their "job interview" of a potential assassin. That they happily accepted commissions to murder retired government operatives like Redmond, Bethke, Grosso and Lang just made it worse.

Bolan brought the Escort to a halt and turned off the ignition. He was about five minutes early for his appointment with Galloway, which was just enough time to check over his armament.

Unburdened by the security of a gun show, the Executioner was fully armed with a Mark XIX .357 Magnum Desert Eagle pistol, a 9 mm SIG-Sauer P-226 handgun and an RRA Tactical Entry 5.56 mm rifle. He checked the clips of all three in succession, making sure they were fully loaded and that he had spare ammo for all three.

Of course, if his recon of the park earlier that morning was any indication, he wouldn't be given much opportunity to reload.

The Executioner wasn't surprised that the Black Cross's notion of a job interview was to send several people to try to kill him. If they succeeded, he wouldn't get the job, and as an added bonus, what little he knew about them would die with him.

If they didn't succeed, he was worthy of being an elite assassin. From the perspective of the Black Cross, it was win-win.

Bolan assumed that the six people hiding in the nearby trees, whom he'd noticed during his earlier recon, were there to perform that task. They likely weren't actual Black Cross assassins—Bolan couldn't imagine that they'd stay in business long if their top assassins' lives were being so easily thrown away on something like this—but mercenaries hired to see if Michael Burns was Black Cross material. Three were up in the trees, the others on the ground.

While Bolan didn't kill innocents, he didn't think anyone who killed a stranger for pay qualified as such.

Though it was sunny and warm, it was still a bit chillier than it had been the day before, a cold wind coming in off the Delaware River, which worked in the Executioner's favor. He was able to holster the rifle on a strap sewn inside the right-hand side of his fleece jacket, which he left unzipped. A similar strap on the left secured the Desert Eagle, with the SIG-Sauer in a Safariland 1060 shoulder holster that fit snugly next to the Kevlar bulletproof vest.

Opening the door of the Escort, Bolan climbed out and closed the door behind him, but didn't lock it. One of the modifications Stony Man had arranged to have made to the vehicle was a bulletproof body and windows. He wanted the option of being able to open the door and use it as a shield once the firing started, as it inevitably would.

Bolan took up position against the car's hood, waiting for Galloway to make his appearance.

For a brief moment, he simply enjoyed the quiet, the smell of the freshly cut grass, the feel of the light breeze, the warmth of the sun on his stubble-covered face. For years Bolan's life had been dedicated solely to the pursuit of those who broke the law while sitting from a lofty place above it, avoiding judgment for their acts. His life as Justice's proxy left him with little time for indulgences such as enjoying a warm spring day.

But this day, for seven minutes, he was able to do so. He had to admit to enjoying the respite.

At eight minutes past noon, though, a battered old Citroën Evasion pulled up behind the Escort, and Galloway bounded out, ending the reprieve. Bolan straightened up—it was time once again for the Executioner to go to work.

"Michael! Glad to see you were able to make it."

Again affecting Michael Burns's Alabama accent, Bolan said, "Well, your offer was powerful temptin', Galloway. So what's the next step?"

"We *step* into the field. Some people from the organization want to get a look at you. They're waiting in there." Galloway pointed a single finger at the small clearing across the street. That clearing was surrounded by the trees where the Executioner knew the half-dozen mercs were waiting for him.

However, while Bolan knew what was coming, Michael Burns didn't. So he followed where Galloway was pointing.

Up to a point, anyhow. He crossed North Gulph and walked about three steps into the grass when he saw a glint of metal being reflected by the sun just at the edge of the tree line, about twenty feet up an oak. The Executioner knew that an assassin was positioned there, and thanks to the telltale glint, so now could Michael Burns. In fact, if Burns was to be considered for membership in the Black Cross, he'd be expected to recognize the glint of metal for what it was.

Certainly, this was further evidence that the six men in the trees *weren't* Black Cross. They couldn't be as successful as they apparently were if they made such amateur mistakes as being in a position to allow their weaponry to reflect sunlight.

Falling forward onto the grass while pulling out his Desert Eagle, Bolan cried, "Ambush!" and fired three .357 rounds at the metal glint.

SITTING IN THE OAK was Dewey Roby, who was grateful that the damn target had finally shown the hell up. Roby was more than happy to take that hot Russian chick's money, but he didn't realize he'd have to sit in a tree for quite this long. His legs were cramping up, and he was thirsty, having already drunk both bottles of water he brought along.

Still, this was the job, and the Russian chick had paid half up front, so Roby was willing to sit in a tree for a few hours with his 7.62 mm WASR-10 rifle—especially since he hadn't actually paid off the WASR-10 yet. A buddy got him a good deal on the Kalashnikov knockoff, but it still wasn't cheap, and Roby just got fired *again,* so he had serious cash flow issues.

Roby planned to show them all—those jackasses in the Army, and the cops and the Feds. Wouldn't take him 'cause he had "socialization issues," whatever the hell *that* meant.

He'd show them all.

Then the target dived to the ground yelling and whipped out a pistol firing it right at Roby.

"Shit!" was the only word he was able to get out as three bullets whistled through the air. The first smashed into his left arm, pulverizing muscle and splintering bone, sending shards of pain cascading throughout Roby's entire body.

The second and third both ripped into the branch he was settled on, sending splinters of wood flying while Roby plummeted to the earth, landing with a bone-jarring impact.

Luckily, Roby was right-handed and managed to squeeze the trigger of his WASR-10. Unluckily, he was in a tangle on the ground and wasn't properly braced to handle the recoil. His shots went flying off in all directions, and the rifle itself rammed into his wounded arm. Roby screamed in agony.

The Executioner kept his head down as the rifle rounds fired randomly. With the man down and wounded, he wasn't an immediate threat, so Bolan focused on the other five. The hitters in the trees were the primary concern, since height gave them an advantage—plus they were less likely to have moved in the past few hours. First Bolan aimed his Desert Eagle at a large maple.

JIMMY FREDERICKS loved his AK-47 so much that he had named it "Vera." It was the same name that a TV show character gave to his favorite gun, and Fredericks always liked that show. He couldn't remember the name of the series, but he knew the guy had a goatee, which Fredericks only remembered because he'd grown one himself so he'd look like the guy. At least he thought he did. It was hard to say with all the different meds he was on. They messed with his head. That was why he took this job, to pay for the meds. Without them, he'd be in even worse shape.

Fredericks took aim at his target, who was lying on the ground, and fired.

BULLETS SLAPPED into the ground around the Executioner from Fredericks's AK-47, some getting painfully close. Bolan loosed another volley from his Desert Eagle, the bullets shearing off the maple branch, sending Fredericks to the ground as quickly as Roby had gone. However, Fredericks went down headfirst, and as soon as his skull impacted with the ground, driving the vertebrae of his neck straight up into his mouth and brainpan, he died instantly.

While Fredericks fell, Bolan turned his head ninety degrees and fired at the third gunner perched in a tree. The mercenary had pushed aside the leaves of the weeping willow he'd taken refuge in so he could get a clear shot with his 5.56 mm Smith & Wesson M&P15T rifle.

PAUL MARKINSON was glad the target had finally arrived, as he still had half-a-dozen errands to run before going home. His wife would *kill* him if he didn't stop off at Costco. So he took aim with the S&W he'd gotten from a cop buddy of his who insisted that the department wouldn't miss one lousy SWAT rifle. Even while wearing the Ray-Ban sunglasses his wife got him because she thought he looked sexy in them, he had no trouble picking up the target, and firing.

SINCE MARKINSON'S position put him perpendicular to Bolan, he fired at the Executioner's torso, which saved Bolan's life. The bullets rammed into his Kevlar, but did not penetrate. The pain of a cracked rib was nothing to Bolan, and he was able to handle the impact with the consummate ease of long practice as he fired back.

The .357 round cracked through the right lens of the Ray-Ban sunglasses, pulped Markinson's right eyeball and pulverized his frontal lobe, ripping out the back of his head.

All that transpired over the course of a few seconds, but the Executioner no longer had the element of surprise. He knew it would be much more difficult to deal with the remaining three mercs.

Feeling more than a little exposed in the clearing, Bolan holstered the Desert Eagle and unhooked the RRA rifle. Flicking the safety to automatic as he clambered to his feet, he braced the rifle stock against his shoulder and fired in an arc at the tree line even as he backed toward the Escort. While he was hoping to hit someone, his main objective was to bang off cover fire to enable him to get to the relative safety of the Escort, giving him cover from the car as his foes had from the trees—though his cover had the advantage of being bulletproof.

Roby chose that moment to finally get to his feet, trying to ignore the white-hot agony in his left arm, and raise his WASR-10 to fire. Unfortunately, he got up right in the path of the spray of bullets from Bolan's RRA rifle, which cut through his entire torso, pulping his internal organs in an instant. He was dead before he fell back to the ground.

Bolan didn't stop firing until he got to the Escort, then he ducked behind it. He heard bullets fly a second after he ceased fire, impacting either with the pavement of North Gulph Road or with the Escort's body. The Executioner took a moment to replace the clips in both the Desert Eagle and the RRA, all the while listening for where the bullets were coming from.

He also noticed that Galloway was nowhere to be seen.

The highest-caliber rounds were striking the front of the Escort, as they were hitting hard enough to dent even the special metal of the car's body. The other two sets of bullets were evenly spaced also, indicating that the three mercs were at ten o'clock, twelve o'clock and two o'clock, relative to his position.

Since what sounded like .50-caliber rounds were coming from the ten-o'clock position—whereas the other two seemed to be simple 9 mm—Bolan thought that the heavy-duty rifleman needed to be taken out first.

The .50-caliber fire was coming continuously, so Bolan knew the man's clip would run dry soon. Once that happened, the Executioner would break cover enough so that he could fire the RRA over the engine block.

THE MAN IN QUESTION, U. L. Gordon, had been half-convinced that the guy they were supposed to shoot was never going to show, so when he did arrive and then took three guys out in about half a second, he had to admit to being impressed.

Gripping his .50 Action Express Desert Eagle tightly, he fired round after round, pausing only briefly after each shot due to the considerable recoil. Still, Gordon was used to it. He'd been using this particular gun for over ten years now, and it had served him well during that time. This guy may have been good enough to take out those three rednecks in the trees, but Gordon was a professional. The target would be toast, Gordon would get the rest of the money from the Russian bitch, and he could go home and celebrate by opening the Chianti Classico. Or maybe the Merlot.

First he had a job to do.

To his surprise, though, the .50-caliber rounds—which should have cut through the target's car like it was tissue paper—weren't even penetrating. Gordon kept firing anyhow, since it was still likely he'd get through eventually, but he was a little pissed that nobody told him he'd be going against a guy with an armored car. Worse, an armored *Escort,* for Christ's sake, which meant the guy was probably a spook of some kind.

Or maybe just another rich white guy who'd tricked out his ride. Gordon didn't really care all that much, as long as the target got dead and he got paid.

Once he fired off the last shot in the chamber, he took refuge behind the oak he'd been using for cover and ejected the empty clip, letting it drop to the dirt.

BOLAN QUICKLY RESTED the RRA on the bullet-ridden hood of the Escort and fired it at the tree that Gordon had taken shelter behind. The bullets chipped away at the old oak, but Gordon had picked his cover well: the tree was thick and tough.

Reaiming his sights lower, Bolan fired again. The rounds tore through the hiking boot on Gordon's right foot, which he had stupidly left exposed. Normally, Gordon wouldn't have been concerned, but the car should have been a clue that this guy was better than most. That realization came too late, as rifle shots mangled the flesh and bones of his right foot, and Gordon fell to the ground, screaming in agony.

Slamming the fresh clip into his Desert Eagle, he blinked away the tears that formed from the destruction of his foot and tried to fire back.

Unfortunately for him, by falling to the ground he left his head and torso in the Executioner's sight line, and he was already aiming toward ground level. Bolan squeezed off several more rounds, and the bullets smashed into Gordon's face and neck and chest. Within moments, there wasn't much left of him above chest level.

AS SOON AS Harry Johannsen had seen his target fall to the ground screaming "Ambush!" he had started firing. Or, rather, squeezing the trigger. The Remington 700 jammed on him. He managed to clear it, but by then, his mark was hiding behind the Escort. Johannsen fired anyhow, figuring he'd cut through that little car's bodywork in short order.

But that didn't work. He called out to Jake West, his partner, who was behind a different tree. "Keep goin'! Son of a bitch has an armored car!"

West had a Remington 700 of his own, but his didn't jam by virtue of West actually remembering to clean the weapon. Johannsen kept *saying* he'd clean it, but he never actually got around to *doing* that. It drove West up the *wall*.

West stopped firing after a few minutes, when he knew he was low on ammo, and rammed home a fresh magazine. Johannsen kept going until his weapon cycled dry. While he reloaded, West kept firing, since by the time his clip was out, Johannsen would have reloaded.

BOLAN WENT BACK behind the car, having finished another magazine from the RRA. The last two mercs continued to fire, sometimes one, sometimes both. Sooner or later, even Stony Man's specially modified Escort was just going to be a twisted pile of pockmarked metal, so there was only so long the Executioner could count on it for cover.

Loading a third clip into the RRA, he risked surfacing long enough to fire off a few rounds before ducking back behind the car. He did so from the roof this time.

The rounds he fired clipped the tree a merc was using for cover, but missed him entirely.

JOHANNSEN AIMED to fire back—but his Remington jammed *again*. Frustrated, he pulled out his backup weapon, a Glock 17, and squeezed off several rounds.

Those shots went nowhere near the target, though. The target resurfaced over the car's trunk this time, firing another burst of shots—one of which struck Johannsen in the shoulder, smashing his clavicle.

Johannsen fell backward, wincing in agony.

From a few feet away, West, still squeezing off rounds

from his own Remington, said, "Goddammit, Harry, I *told* you to wear the goddamn vest, goddammit!"

Again, the mark popped up, this time over the hood again, and was able to take proper aim at Johannsen, the rifle rounds tearing his torso to pieces, shredding his ribs and heart in an instant.

West couldn't believe what he saw. He and Johannsen had been partners for fifteen years now. They first met in Iraq in 1992 during the first Gulf War, when they both served as Marines. After their tours ended, they decided to go into business for themselves, and had done well as guns for hire all over the world. They'd just gotten back from a job in Angola, and were in town for the gun show when that Russian lady hired them. They hadn't even intended to do any work for a while—the trip to the gun show was supposed to be a vacation before heading home to Fort Wayne—but the money was too good.

And now Johannsen was dead. Fifteen years of fighting together with barely a scratch, and now one man just killed him on a job they took as a lark.

West wasn't about to let that stand. Hefting his Remington, he broke cover and started firing at Bolan, screaming, "You goddamn son of a bitch, you killed Harry! Goddammit, you're gonna goddamn *die* for this, you goddamn hear me? Huh?"

Bolan ignored the man's screaming, instead ducking back behind the Escort, and waiting for West to empty his clip.

As soon as the Remington started dry firing, the Executioner pulled out his SIG-Sauer and fired at West, who was now standing in the middle of the clearing in front of the tree line. The 9 mm bullet drilled into West's left cheek and sliced into the brain stem causing him to die instantly. He fell to the ground, still dry firing the Remington, the bullet lodged in the back of his head.

"Well done."

Bolan leaped to his feet, whirled, and aimed his SIG-Sauer at the voice that seemingly came out of nowhere. Somehow, an attractive brunette managed to get the drop on him in the middle of a firefight, which was no mean feat.

In Burns's Alabama accent, he asked, "Where's Galloway at?"

In an obvious Russian accent, though light enough to indicate that she'd been speaking English regularly for over a decade, the woman answered, "Mr. Galloway has served his function. I am Ms. White, and I am empowered to offer you a place in the Black Cross."

5

Allen Bradlee had a very set routine. Every day, he went in to work at the National Security Agency headquarters in Fort Meade, Maryland, where he worked as a deputy director, at 8:30 a.m. precisely. He checked traffic patterns to make sure that he would not be late, and the only time he was ever tardy was when either he had a meeting outside the office, or when an unforeseen traffic issue occurred.

At precisely noon he would go to lunch, barring unforeseen circumstances, get into his car and drive south on the Baltimore-Washington Parkway to Route 198, where there was a delicatessen that made perfect Reuben sandwiches. He'd order a Reuben and a root beer, sit down with the *Washington Post,* and read it for half-an-hour before driving back up the parkway to the office.

Bradlee prided himself on having very few weaknesses—his fondness for a good Reuben was the only one he was willing to admit to.

On his way out the door, he'd wish his secretary, Glynis, well, and ask if she needed him to get anything for her. She always said no, but thanked him for the consideration. Considering how much of what

Bradlee did was to look for patterns in people's conversations and actions, he always found it amusing that he and Glynis had such discernible and predictable patterns.

This day was a typical day, at first. He got in at 8:30 a.m., did his morning work, left at noon, asked Glynis if she wanted anything, drove down to Route 198, ate his Reuben, read the *Post* and returned to the office.

When he got back, Glynis said that he had received a phone call from General Spencer, which she had sent to his voice mail.

Bradlee sighed. Calls from General Spencer always meant a disruption to the routine.

He entered his office, closed the door behind him, sat down at his immaculately neat desk and looked at the phone. The red light over the button with a drawing of an envelope on it was lit, meaning he had voice mail. He picked up the receiver, pushed that button and was told he had three voice mail messages.

Skipping and saving the first two once he realized they weren't Spencer, he then listened to the third.

"Allen, she's at it again. The whole thing's going to be *seriously* compromised if she keeps this up. She's already got two senators and half the damn House committee going along with her nonsense. She needs to be stopped, Allen, and I mean *now*. It's your mess—clean it up."

Bradlee sighed. He played the message a second time, then erased it.

After staring at the phone for several seconds, Bradlee then pulled out his BlackBerry and called up a phone number in the directory under the name Higby's Imports and Exports.

He entered the number on his cell phone, hesitated, then pressed Talk.

"Higby's I and E," said the voice on the other end.

"Sorry, wrong number."

Bradlee pressed End, then waited.

Within thirty seconds, his cell phone rang, the words Blocked Caller ID came up on the display.

Again, he pushed Talk.

"The job we discussed?" he said without preamble.

"Yes?" said the voice on the other end, which belonged to a man that Bradlee knew only as "Mr. Indigo."

"It's a go."

"When the money is transferred into our account, *then* it's a go, Mr. Bradlee."

Bradlee nodded, even though Indigo couldn't see that. "Of course."

With that, Bradlee ended the conversation. He had been hoping to avoid this, of course, but Spencer's call made that impossible. She wouldn't listen to reason. So she had to go. That was all there was to it.

He dialed another number, this one an international call to a Cayman Islands bank. Using the BlackBerry, he called up two sets of numbers, neither of which were labeled in the BlackBerry itself, but Bradlee knew what they each were: account numbers. One for a discretionary NSA fund that only five people in the agency knew about—three four-stars, another deputy director and Bradlee. Speaking in halting French, he requested a transfer from that account to the account corresponding to the other number.

When that was finished, he erased each of the last

three calls from his cell phone log. Then he reopened his office door.

"Mr. McDowell wants to have a word with you," Glynis said.

Letting out a long sigh, Bradlee composed himself and said, "Of course. Tell him to come on by."

The Black Cross would take care of General Spencer's little problem.

**6**

Bolan drove around Humboldt County for several hours after losing the tail that the Black Cross put on him. The organization probably wasn't going to be pleased at his shaking it. On the other hand, it likely was another test, like the mercs in Valley Forge National Historical Park—if he could lose the tail, he was worthy of being in the Black Cross.

Once safely away from the tail, Bolan took out his sat phone. Within minutes, after the signal bounced through a series of cutouts, he was talking to Brognola. He spoke openly, despite the slight risk, since he had no idea when or even if a face-to-face would be possible while the op was ongoing, and he needed to touch base with the head of Stony Man sooner rather than later.

"Striker," Brognola said when they were connected. "Are you in?"

"So far. After the park, they flew me to their compound in Northern California, though it won't be their compound for much longer. They move around, and nobody knows where the next location will be. In fact, it wouldn't surprise me if they've picked it."

"And it's definitely the Black Cross?" Brognola

almost sounded excited. He was too professional to truly be eager, but he came as close as he ever was likely to.

"That's what they call themselves. After I took down the assassins in Valley Forge, a woman who called herself Ms. White said she represented them. She gave me a flight to be on at Philadelphia International, which took me to Eureka/Arcata, and a chopper took me from there. I met the head, a man named Mr. Indigo. From now on, I'm to be called Mr. Sapphire."

"No real names?"

"No. And I didn't recognize White or Indigo."

Brognola knew that was not just an idle comment. Bolan had a phenomenal memory, and if he'd seen Indigo or White in a mug book or computer file at any point, he'd recognize them now.

The Executioner continued, "They also are apparently down to only six assassins—seven, counting me. They're trying to get their fighting strength up to a dozen."

"Only a dozen?" Brognola was stunned. Given what the Black Cross had been able to accomplish, he had expected a much larger group.

"Since they're at half strength, they should be easier to take down," Bolan said. "Oh, and Indigo said that they'd vetted me pretty thoroughly, and that the park was a test of my combat skills—I surpassed expectations. So tell the Bear that he did his work well."

"I will. And just to reassure you, I've looked into the six bodies that turned up in the park, and all six of them had felony warrants out on them—four for murder. The other two were Dewey Roby and U. L. Gordon."

Bolan recognized one of those names. "Isn't Gordon the one responsible for those killings in Malawi?"

"Absolutely, but we've never been able to prove it—and neither has Interpol."

"What about Roby?"

"He's a soldier-and-cop wannabe who only isn't wanted for murder by virtue of never hitting what he was aiming at. He's wanted for assault with a deadly weapon for several gunshot wounds he's inflicted."

"Good." The Executioner had no compunctions about killing people who fired weapons at him, but he felt better about it knowing that they were criminals and murderers. "They gave me a cell phone that they'll call me on when they're ready to use me on a job. It'll be as part of a team—turns out most of their jobs are team efforts, which explains how well they clean up after themselves."

"Impressive," Brognola said. "Paid assassins aren't known for working well with others."

"They are when they're paid well enough," Bolan said. "Indigo promised seven-figure takes on most jobs."

"That can certainly buy cooperation, yes." Brognola sighed. "All right, Striker. Best not to contact me again until you have something solid."

"Agreed."

A breeting sound came from the phone in Bolan's coat pocket.

"That's my new employer now," Bolan said. "I'll talk to you later."

After disconnecting, Bolan retrieved the fliptop cell phone and opened it. The display gave a number with a 707 area code. Pushing the Talk button, Bolan spoke in "Mr. Sapphire's" accent. "That was a lousy tail y'all put on me, there," he said without preamble. "I like my privacy."

The deep, resonant voice of Mr. Indigo sounded in the earpiece. "Consider it the final part of the interview, Mr. Sapphire. We learned of your talents in the killing arts at Valley Forge. We also wanted to test your more covert skills."

"Well, you done went and tested them. Oh, and I took the tracker out of the cell phone, too, and put on a scrambler, so don't go tryin' to triangulate nothin'. What's next?"

"Now we want you to return to HQ."

"I just left there!" Bolan sounded indignant. "Make up your minds, will ya?"

"A job just came up that will be a good field test for you."

"Oh yeah? Peachy. I'll be there in three hours." In fact, he was only two hours from the cabin in the Redwood forest, but he didn't need Indigo to know that.

THREE HOURS LATER, the Executioner, aka "Mr. Sapphire," returned to the cabin. Besides Mr. Indigo, there was a young man who sat at a laptop that was hooked into a huge flat-screen monitor. The young man was practically bouncing in his chair.

Three more people entered the room. One was Ms. White. Another was a muscular African-American man with receding close-cropped hair and a thick mustache. He wore a plain black T-shirt that accentuated his cut chest, a well-worn leather jacket over it, black jeans and black cowboy boots.

The last was an older woman with glasses on a chain around her neck, and paper-white hair. She wore a gray cardigan sweater over a white button-down blouse, and a midcalf-length plaid skirt. Bolan suspected that she cultivated the look of a saintly old grandmother, but he watched her walk into the room and knew instantly that she was as well trained as any of them. Her well-muscled legs were visible under the skirt, and the air of relaxed confidence was something Bolan had only seen in people with serious combat training.

"Welcome," Indigo said. "Let me introduce you all." He pointed at each of them in turn. "Mr. Pink, Ms. Orange, Ms. White and Mr. Sapphire."

Keeping in character for the good old boy he was posing as, Bolan looked at the large African-American man and said, "Mr. Pink, huh?"

"Last time a man joked about that, it was the last joke he ever made, you feel me, cracker?" Then he smiled. "'Sides, least I ain't no piece of ladies jewelry."

Indigo held up a hand before Bolan could reply. "That's enough! Mr. Sapphire, you know why we—"

"Yeah, yeah," Bolan said. "We gotta stay anonymous even to each other, fine. I was just razzin' the fella, nothin' to get crazy about." He looked at Pink. "I didn't mean nothin' by it, Mr. Pink. I'm sure it'll be an honor to work with ya."

Folding his large arms over his wide chest, Pink said, "Yeah, I bet it will be for you."

Rolling her eyes, White asked impatiently, "Can we get on with this, please?"

"Of course, Ms. White," Indigo said, pausing to glare at both Pink and Bolan with his wide brown eyes, before nodding to the young man at the laptop, who typed some keys. "This is the job for the four of you."

The flat-screen monitor lit up with the image of a light-skinned African-American woman with her hair in twists, large brown eyes, with dark freckles under those eyes.

"This is Ami Pembleton," Indigo continued. "She's a lobbyist in D.C. who lives in Baltimore, and the client wants her eliminated. Her husband's a detective in the Check and Fraud Unit of the Baltimore Police Department, plus, like any good lobbyist, she has a lot of friends on Capitol Hill."

Bolan noted that Indigo did not reveal who the client was, nor the reasons why Pembleton was being targeted. He suspected that such information would not be forthcoming, and if he asked for it, it would jeopardize his cover.

Instead, he asked, "You need four of us for this?"

"Yes. For one thing, there's the BPD connection. Cops have a tendency to seek retribution against deaths in their house, as it were."

Bolan shrugged. "I guess."

For the first time, Orange spoke. "No 'guessing' about it, young man. It's my experience that officers of the law tend to take their vendettas very seriously—and the death of an officer, or of an officer's family, inevitably leads to a vendetta."

"So what's your job in this one, Granny?" Bolan asked with a deliberately obnoxious grin. "You gonna check out the library books we need to study up on this lady?"

Before Orange had a chance to respond, Pink got right into Bolan's face. "You *want* me to kick your ass, don't ya?"

"No," Bolan said, not giving in, "I wanna know who I'm runnin' with. White here got the drop on me when we first met, so I know what she's bringin' to the table.

You obviously got muscle, so I figure you'll be doin'
the heavy liftin'. And I know what *I* can do. But Ms.
Orange here is just some old lady. Out there, we're
dependin' on each other to survive, and I wanna know
what I'm dependin' on."

Orange was smiling now, looking for all the world
like a sweet old grandmother giving candy to her grand-
kids. "Try and grab me, young man."

Bolan knew that as soon as he tried to do so, she'd
take him down, but since "Mr. Sapphire" wasn't
expected to, he played along and lunged toward her.

Two seconds later, he was on the floor, on his back,
her flat-heeled right shoe pressed into his chest. She
had used a fairly standard judo throw, but she
executed it perfectly. Normally, Bolan would have
deflected the throw, but the need to stay in character
forced him to go against his instincts. However, even
if he had tried to resist, it might not have worked—
she was *that* good.

Still with the sweet smile, she asked, "Any other
questions?"

Grinning widely, Bolan asked, "Yeah—what the hell
you need the rest of us for?"

That got her to provide a somewhat more genuine
smile. "I need someone to fetch my tea."

"With or without milk?"

"Without. Two sugars."

"All right," Indigo said, "that's enough. Ms. Orange,
please let Mr. Sapphire up."

Not only did Orange remove her foot, but she held out
a hand to Bolan. Out of curiosity as much as anything,
he accepted the hand. She pulled him to his feet with far

greater ease than one would expect from a "little old lady," and he could feel the calluses on her hands.

The Executioner made a note of it. Her affect made her the most dangerous person in the room, because she was the easiest to underestimate just by looking at her. Even now, knowing how strong and capable she was, Bolan's instinct was to dismiss her out of hand.

He needed to be careful of that.

Indigo continued, "The second reason why this requires four of you is Pembleton's friends on the Hill. In certain circles, she's well-known and well-liked, and people in those circles have a lot of suction. Her death needs to hold up against a thorough investigation— which is where we come in."

Turning his intense eyes on the attractive young woman, he went on. "Ms. White's the coordinator. She'll lead the op and make the calls in the field. Everything goes through her, is that understood?"

Each person nodded—except White, naturally.

The young man leaped up from the laptop and handed each assassin a manila envelope.

"Those are your plane tickets and hotel itineraries. Do *not* share them with each other. Also in there are disposable cell phones, which are only to be used to contact each other. Three of you also have had half your fee transferred to your bank accounts. The transfer receipt's in the folder as well." Indigo looked at Bolan. "The exception is you."

While the Executioner couldn't have cared less about the dirty money he was getting from these people, he had a cover to maintain. "Why the hell's that?"

"This is your first op. You haven't proved a damn

thing to any one of us. This is your chance. You make it through okay, you do what Ms. White tells you to do and you contribute to making the op go smoothly—and you survive the experience—then you'll get the entire fee when it's over. If for any reason we decide that you haven't lived up to that, then you'll be terminated."

"Assuming," Pink added, "you don't get your ass killed in the field." Pink's tone indicated he'd be happy to be the one to do so.

Indigo looked at each of them in turn. "All of you will leave here in sequence. First Ms. White, then Mr. Pink, then Ms. Orange and lastly Mr. Sapphire. Ms. White will contact you via text message on the disposables once you're all in the D.C. area."

Without another word, White left the room.

"What're we supposed to do in the meanwhile?" Bolan asked.

"Keep a low profile," Indigo said. "Do nothing to make yourself stand out from the crowd. Don't be a recluse in your hotel room, but don't make your movements obvious, either. Don't—"

"Yeah, yeah," Bolan said impatiently, "I got that. I mean while we wait for you to let us go."

The kid at the laptop spoke for the first time. "We got snacks."

Bolan rolled his eyes.

After ten minutes, Pink left. Orange then said to Bolan, "You should know, I'm a third-degree black belt in judo. Nobody's ever been able to grab me in the thirty years since I got to that *kyu*."

"Good to know," Bolan said.

That was Orange's first mistake. By actually stating

her proficiency level, it made her seem like more of a real threat. The Executioner already knew that, but he planned to make her eat those words.

After Indigo released Orange, he looked right at Bolan. "This is your final test, Mr. Sapphire. Ami Pembleton will be dead when this is over, and there'll be no evidence of how or why she was killed. If that *isn't* the result, you won't live to regret it. Am I clear?"

"Crystal," Bolan said.

Someone wouldn't live to regret it, but it wasn't going to be him.

## 7

Knowing that the op was going to be slow, deliberate and planned, Bolan did not risk contacting Stony Man with what he knew until after he had landed at Ronald Reagan Washington National Airport and had checked into the airport hotel room that the Black Cross had reserved for him under the name "John Sapphire." Even then, on the off chance that White or one of the others was in this hotel and checking up on him, he spent some time in the hotel bar, nursing non-alcoholic beer for a couple of hours, engaging in meaningless small talk with a very bored bartender and making sure there was nobody watching him.

Finally, satisfied that he wasn't being observed, he went back to his room and only then did he take out the sat phone. No doubt, they weren't concerned with what he did before White's text message told them to meet. If he didn't show, they hadn't lost anything—they hadn't paid "Mr. Sapphire," he knew none of their names, and he doubted the Humboldt County retreat would be in use for much longer.

As soon as he was put through to Brognola, Bolan said, "We've got a problem. First target is a lobbyist named Ami Pembleton."

"I know her," Brognola said, to Bolan's lack of surprise. From what Indigo said, Pembleton was an influential lobbyist, and there wasn't anybody inside the Beltway who could be labeled "influential" that Brognola *didn't* know.

Bolan provided the information that was in the manila envelope given to him by the hyperactive young man at the laptop. "One of her clients is MJN."

"I know the story, Striker," Brognola said.

McNamara Johnson Norville was a major Department of Defense contractor that, ten years earlier, had been beaten out by Fuster & Son for the construction of a new troop transport for use in the desert. The contract called for a transport vehicle that would be ready for testing in five years. In double that time, they had nothing to show for the contract, except billions of dollars spent in R&D. Every scheduled field test had been postponed, most at the last minute, and the transport had yet to be deployed even in a simulation. MJN, who had successfully executed dozens of contracts for the DOD without anything remotely resembling the problems Fuster was having with the transport vehicle, hired Pembleton to try to convince the members of the Senate and House Armed Services Committees to investigate Fuster.

And she was having some luck. Several senators and congresspeople were asking questions, ones that neither the Pentagon nor anyone at Fuster were in a great hurry to answer.

"There's no information as to who the client is," Bolan said. "But my guess would be someone in the DOD, or maybe NSA or CIA—or someone at Fuster."

"Or all of the above," Brognola said. "Given what the Black Cross charges for its services, this could be a team effort."

"Yeah. Pembleton's husband is a BPD detective, so part of our mission profile involves keeping him out of it. We need to fake killing her and set her up at a safehouse until this blows over."

"I assume you can handle the first part."

"Absolutely," the Executioner said with assuredness.

"Fine. I know the safehouse in Brady's Bend is free. I'll make sure it stays that way. But I don't have anybody available for protection. Best I can do is some marshals."

"All right, but I want to vet the marshals you do use," Bolan said.

"Of course. I'll have a list for you by tomorrow."

"No rush—it'll be a few days before I even know what the Black Cross's game plan is. I won't be able to put together a profile for the op until I know what Ms. White has in mind."

Right after hanging up with Brognola, Bolan got a text message from the Black Cross that read: The Horowitz birthday party will be at the Bell & Whistle on J St. tomorrow night at 7:30.

Bolan was pleased things were moving forward. For now he would get a good night's sleep. The following day he would be ready for the next phase of his mission and one step closer to eliminating the Black Cross.

**8**

The Bell & Whistle was a dingy bar on J Street that seemed to cater to a group of regulars. On this weeknight, the place was empty of all save a few older men who looked as if life had beaten them down rather thoroughly, and a few older women who looked as if they were trying too hard to get picked up.

Walking up to the bar, having arrived right at seven-thirty, Bolan put on his accent and said, "I'm here for the Horowitz party?"

The bartender, a young man with spiky hair and a toothpick in his mouth who was cleaning a pint glass, indicated the area to his right with his head. He was wearing a black muscle shirt with a white line-drawing of the bar's facade and the words Bell & Whistle under the artwork, and green pants.

Following this prompt, Bolan looked to his left to see a dark, narrow staircase. He approached it, noticing that the wooden stairs had long since warped and shifted so that the distance between stairs wasn't the same from one step to the next, and each of them creaked loudly.

Once he got upstairs and turned left, he saw a series of tables, only one of which had anyone seated at it.

White and Orange were already there, sitting opposite each other at a four-person table, both with drinks in hand, and a manila envelope between them in the center of the table. White was wearing a red sweatshirt with the words Washington D.C. emblazoned across her rather prodigious chest. Even through the miasma of sweat and booze that permeated the Bell & Whistle, Bolan could smell the chemicals on the shirt, indicating it hadn't been washed. She had probably just bought it that day. Ditto the jeans that hugged her long legs.

As for Orange, she wore a blue blouse and a brown cardigan, and had replaced the plaid skirt with a pair of loose-fitting khaki slacks.

White had a shot glass with a clear liquid that Bolan assumed to be either tequila or vodka—the latter was more likely, given her obvious Russian heritage, but Bolan didn't like to make assumptions. Orange had a mug with a string hanging over the edge, indicating that it was tea.

He walked up to the table and said, "No milk, two sugars, right?"

Orange smiled. "Good memory."

"I always 'member the important stuff."

White regarded him. "Let us hope so, Mr. Sapphire."

"Don't worry your pretty little head 'bout it. Where's Pinko?"

"Right behind you."

The Executioner whirled to see Pink come to the top of the staircase. He was wearing the same leather jacket and cowboy boots, but this time both his T-shirt and jeans were a dark blue.

"Have a seat, gentlemen," White said.

Indicating the chair on White's right with an exaggerated flourish, Bolan said, "After you, Mr. Pink."

Pink scowled at the Executioner, but took the seat. Bolan, who sat opposite Pink on White's left, knew that he'd be able to take down Orange by pulling the lady's own trick on her—letting her think he wasn't as good as he really was. Pink, he'd be able to deal with by pissing him off enough that he'd do something stupid.

That left White. Bolan hadn't figured out how to take care of her.

Yet.

And then, of course, there were the other three, assuming there were no other new recruits, plus Indigo. Bolan was less concerned about support staff and the like. The important part was eliminating the killers.

A waitress came up the stairs, wearing a black T-shirt that was of the same design as the bartender's muscle shirt, and similar green pants. "What do you guys want?" she asked.

"Pint of whatever y'all have on tap," Bolan said.

The waitress glared at him. "We have five beers on tap."

In fact, they only had three tap handles at the bar that, along with the waitress's not having a pad to write things down on, made Bolan concerned for her ability to do her job, but he just let loose with a good old boy grin and said, "Surprise me, darlin'."

She rolled her eyes, then looked at Pink. "And you?"

"JD on the rocks."

Frowning, the waitress said, "JD?"

Pink scowled. "Jack Daniel's."

"Oh, right. 'Kay."

She walked off.

As soon as she disappeared down the stairs, White said, "For now, our job is surveillance. This will continue for the next two weeks in order to determine patterns—or verify ones we have already guessed."

"Two *weeks?*" In fact, Bolan was impressed with their thoroughness, in a disgusted kind of way. "Why so long?"

"Because the Black Cross is a premium assassination service," White said tightly.

"So I'm seein'. I'm more of a point-and-shoot kinda guy."

"When the time is right," White continued, "we will make use of that talent, Mr. Sapphire. But first, we must determine the best way to accomplish our goal without there being any evidence of the assassination."

She pulled a sheet of paper out of the envelope and handed it to Bolan. "This is her address. It is a row house in suburban Baltimore. Your job is to perform discreet surveillance on the residence, determine the habits, not only of Ms. Pembleton, but also of Detective Tim Brabson."

Bolan took the paper. "That the husband?"

White nodded.

"Golly-gee—woman kept her name when she got hitched. That's damned liberated of her."

"In case you ain't noticed, cracker," Pink said, "it's the twenty-*first* century."

"That's what they tell me, Pinko," Bolan said with a grin.

White continued as if he hadn't spoken. "No children as yet, though according to the records of the credit card that the pair of them use for household expenses, they have a cat, who gets regular checkups at the Farstein Veterinary Center."

"Want me to check that out, too?"

"Not unless you see them departing the house with a cat carrier."

Then White pulled another sheet out. "Ms. Orange, a check on her personal credit card, which she uses for business, shows that she regularly eats lunch at the Palace of Japan near Dupont Circle. You are to go there for lunch every day, and determine what she eats, when she eats, and so on."

Orange took the paper but also frowned. "Don't the credit cards tell you that?"

"To an extent, but it is best to have visual confirmation."

Bolan nodded. "Ain't nothin' beats eyeballin' somethin', that's for damn sure."

Pink scowled. "Will you just shut your damn mouth and let the woman *speak?*"

Holding up both hands in an *excuse-me* gesture, the Executioner leaned back in his chair.

"We also need the make and model of her cell phone. Once I know that, I will acquire a duplicate in order to temporarily switch phones so I may place a listening device in hers."

"Sounds good," Pink said.

"Good" was not the word Bolan would have used. The more he heard, the more difficult he realized this would be.

"Mr. Pink," White said, taking out a third sheet, "you are to surveil her place of business on P Street. She does not spend very much time there, but it is her base of operations. When she is not present, go inside on some pretense—perhaps as a messenger—and speak with the support staff. Learn who else works there."

"You got it," Pink said, taking the paper.

The waitress then came back with a Jack Daniel's— straight up—and a pint of beer. She gave Pink the beer and Bolan the shot.

Once she departed, the Executioner pushed the shot glass across the table. "That girl's anglin' for a poor tip."

"Damn right," Pink said, staring dolefully at the iceless shot, but not actually picking it up to drink.

Bolan did take a sip of his beer, which wasn't the worst beer he'd ever had only by virtue of having had some truly piss-poor *chongo* in Mexico years ago.

"Let us get to work, then," White said, as she got up from her chair, tossing a twenty-dollar bill on the table.

9

Ami Pembleton was stunned to realize she didn't have a lunch date, and also had the freedom to take a one-hour lunch.

Originally, she was going to meet with Senator Torvaldsen, but he got called back to Minnesota for a family emergency, and by some strange miracle nobody had jumped in to take the date.

It had been a few weeks since she'd been to Palace of Japan as, for whatever reason, her recent lunch dates expressed a preference for something other than Japanese food. The days she had to work through lunch Lola ordered takeout.

Lunch with Torvaldsen usually required clearing the entire afternoon for that day. The senator was a firm believer in the three-martini lunch, and even when you'd thought he talked your ear off, he was just getting started. As it was now, though, until the meeting with the Global Defense Council at five, she was free.

"I'll be at Palace of Japan," Ami told Lola as she walked out of the office.

Lola smiled. "Asano will fall over from the shock," she said, referring to the restaurant owner.

"Yeah, yeah. The GDC's at five, right?"

"Mmm. What do you think they want?" Lola asked.

Stuffing the hardcover novel that she'd been trying to read for the past ten months into her already over-stuffed Coach bag, Pembleton said, "With luck, they want to give me large sums of money to help get that environmental bill out of committee."

"Large sums of money are good."

"I agree. I'll be back in an hour or so."

"Fine. See you in two hours," Lola said.

Pembleton blinked. "Hey!"

"Ami, in the four years I've been your assistant—with only one raise, by the way, and if GDC gives you those sums of money—"

"Yeah, yeah," Pembleton said, waving Lola off.

"In all those four years, you have *never* spent less than two hours at Palace of Japan. Never happened."

"Bite me entirely, Lola," Pembleton said, and that was her exit line, as the elevator conveniently chose that moment to show up. Pembleton Inc. took up the entire third floor of the old office building, so the elevator simply emptied out into the reception area.

Palace of Japan was only a short walk from the office, and it was actually a nice day. On the morning news, they were predicting rain, so naturally it was sunny and bright without a cloud in the sky.

She walked down P Street to Dupont Circle, crossed it, then walked half a block to the restaurant.

Sure enough, Asano, who was standing at the front station with the maître d', was stunned to see her. "I was starting to think you forgot us."

"Never, Asano, you know that."

"Christina will take you to your table, and I'll have Yoshi start on your sushi deluxe."

"And a Sapporo," she said to Asano's retreating form. If she was going to be dealing with crazed environmentalists later that afternoon, at the very least she wanted a mild beer buzz.

Two-and-a-half hours later, she had downed a fine bowl of miso soup, a delicious plate of sushi, a bowl of green tea ice cream and two Sapporos. Best of all, her cell phone had only rung four times, which was a record low for pretty much any 150-minute period.

She also realized that Lola had been right about the two-hour-plus thing.

With a dramatic sigh, she asked for the check and finished the chapter she'd been reading in her book. While she waited, the phone rang. The display showed the number of one of the Capitol's trunk lines.

"Ami Pembleton."

"Hold for Congressman Whelan."

Pembleton let out a huge grin. Lola had been leaving three messages a day with the congressman.

"Well, hello there, Mrs. Brabson."

She winced at the use of her husband's surname, but let it go. She wanted something from Whelan, and she'd never get it if she corrected him. Whelan was an old-fashioned type from Montana who believed that women should take on their husband's name when they got married, and refused to accept it when they didn't. Whelan also didn't think women belonged in politics.

"To what do I owe this honor, Congressman?"

"Well, my girl tells me that your girl's been making

a nuisance of herself, so I thought maybe I should return the call and find out what all the fuss was over."

The waitress brought back the padded rectangular booklet with her bill. She tossed her business credit card on top of the booklet without even looking at it, and the waitress grabbed both and left.

"You're on the committee, Congressman, I think you know what it's about—assuming you actually *talk* to your fellow committee members."

"Maybe, but I'd still like to hear it from the horse's mouth, so to speak."

"I think the committee needs to investigate Fuster."

"For what, exactly?"

Now she *knew* he was playing dumb. "Congressman, you know as well as I do that the contract called for testing the transport vehicle within five years. That should've happened five years *ago* at the latest."

The waitress brought the booklet back with Pembleton's credit card sticking out of it. She opened the booklet and, looking at the bill's total, did some quick math in her head while the congressman spoke. "Come *on* now, Mrs. Brabson, you know as well as I do that you can't put a timetable on these things."

"Really? Then why is there a timetable *in the contract?*" She wrote down what she was fairly sure amounted to a twenty percent tip in the line under the amount, added that to the total and put it on the line underneath, then signed her name.

"Don't play your little special-interest games with me, young lady. This is just a tempest in a teapot, and that dog won't hunt."

The lobbyist marveled at the congressman's ability

to work three clichés into two sentences like that as she gathered up her purse and jacket and headed toward the door.

Whelan went on, "The good folks at Fuster are just trying to make sure the vehicle is the best available troop transport."

"From the reports I've seen, they're mostly trying to make sure they can keep bilking money out of the Pentagon. They also keep changing the specs every three months. This thing has gone into the billions, Congressman, and they're nowhere near providing a proper troop transport. Maybe you're right, maybe they are being perfectionists, but there's a fine line between that and being incompetent, and at the very least, I think they might be dancing on that line. Look, what's the point of having congressional oversight if you don't occasionally oversee something? I'm not asking you to put the screws to Fuster, I'm asking you to simply do what the committee's supposed to do." By this time, Pembleton was in the restaurant lobby and had found a corner to talk in, since she didn't want to compete with the street noise.

"You see," Whelan said, "this is why I don't like talking to you."

She smiled sweetly, even though the expression was lost over the phone. "Because I make so much sense?"

"Very funny." Whelan exhaled for two seconds. "Look, I'll think about it, all right? Give me two days. And stop having your girl call my girl. She's got *real* work to do."

With that, the congressman ended the call.

Pembleton let out a deep breath as she opened the door. As she walked out, she crashed into someone. Her purse and cell phone both fell to the sidewalk with a clatter, along with a shopping bag, another purse, a book and another cell phone.

"Oh my God, am so sorry," said the woman she'd bumped into. She spoke with a thick Russian accent. "I did not see. Please, am sorry."

"It's okay," Pembleton said, recovering quickly.

"Am so so sorry, did not see," the Russian woman repeated as she knelt to pick up everything. She was wearing a white silk blouse that was unbuttoned at the top two buttons, and still barely contained her rather impressive cleavage. The Russian woman was also wearing a miniskirt and *way* too much makeup.

"It's really okay," she said again.

"Here you go." The Russian woman had a look of panic on her face as she handed Pembleton her purse and cell phone. "Please, am so sorry."

"No worries," Pembleton said as she took her items, quickly dropping the phone into the bag. "I should've been paying better attention. Here, let me help—"

"No, is okay," the Russian woman said quickly before Pembleton could return the favor and help her pick up her own stuff. "Is my fault. Am so so so sorry."

The woman picked up her stuff. Pembleton rolled her eyes as several men walked by and stared openly at the view granted by the woman kneeling in a miniskirt. She was used to that sort of behavior from the male of the species—she *was* married to a cop, after all—but that didn't make it any less revolting.

Once she was sure that the Russian woman had pulled herself together, Pembleton headed back to her office.

To her amazement, she didn't receive even one call on the way back.

However, as soon as she stepped off the elevator, the phone rang.

Lola laughed. "You know, you don't *have* to bring it with you everywhere."

"I do if you want that raise," she said, as she pulled out the phone.

To Pembleton's confusion, the display on the phone had *her* cell phone number on it as the number that was calling her.

"What the hell?" She opened the phone and put it to her ear. "Hello?"

"Am so sorry," said a familiar Russian-accented voice. "I took your phone by mistake. Am so so so sorry."

Briefly, Pembleton moved the phone away from her head and realized that it wasn't actually her phone. Same make and model—she used a fairly standard Motorola fliptop—but now that she looked at it closely, this one didn't have the chip in the metal from the time she dropped it on the Capitol steps.

Quickly, she arranged for the Russian woman to come to her office so they could exchange phones. It was easier that way.

## 10

One week after their meet at the Bell & Whistle, the three Black Cross assassins and the Executioner met at a different bar, this time a Baltimore dive called the Waterfront in Fells Point. It was located across the street from an old warehouse on a street paved with cobblestones.

The service here was far better than it had been at the Bell & Whistle, though there was less privacy. Feeling the tables were too exposed, the four of them took up positions around the pool table in the back.

"Boys versus girls?" Bolan asked with a cheeky grin.

Orange smiled. She was wearing yet another blouse and cardigan combo, this one blue and forest green, respectively. She had also gone back to the plaid skirt. "Fine by me. We'll even let you break."

Pink barked out a laugh. "You let us break, you won't be needin' that stick in your hand. Rack 'em."

Orange started to put the solid and striped balls into the triangle at one end of the table, the eight ball in the middle. Pink chalked up his pool cue. Bolan grabbed a cue and did the same.

While Pink set up his break, White asked, "What did everyone learn?"

In his Southern accent, the Executioner said, "Maid spends more time in that house than Pembleton does. So does the hubby. I'm guessin' the Check and Fraud Unit don't give out much by way of overtime, 'cause he's home at 4:30 p.m. every afternoon—'cept Friday, when he got in late. I figure he was off bendin' his elbow with his buddies."

Pink took a shot, and both the 1-ball and the three ball sank. "Solids for us." He walked around the table, trying to find the best shot to take on the four ball. "Talked with Pembleton's secretary—fine-lookin' woman named Lola. Was there for about half an hour, but only ten minutes of that was actual talking. Girl spent most of her time with the phone at her ear, and it was usually Pembleton on her cell." He sank the four ball in the corner pocket. "Lady spends most of her day in meetings all over town."

"Grabbing her cell phone was the right idea," Orange said. "She's on that thing constantly, based on the one lunch I saw her have. That's a really good restaurant, by the way."

"Thing is," Bolan said, "she works through the weekend, too. This lady don't take no time off."

"Mr. Sapphire is right," Orange said. "She spends most of her time going to different spots within Washington, D.C., most of which are high-security zones like the Capitol, the White House and so on. Her commute takes her on one of the most well-traveled interstates in the country."

Playing along, the Executioner added, "And her house is on a residential street where all the neighbors are all over everywhere. Had a hell of a time doin' surveillance and stayin' hidden from the lookie-loos, ya know?"

"I agree," White said as Pink sank the four ball. "As she goes through the normal course of her daily life, the opportunity to terminate cleanly does not present itself. When I spoke with her upon returning the 'accidentally' switched cell phone, she spoke of how she is so busy that she barely knows which way is up." White frowned.

That got Pink's attention, and he looked up, almost messing up his shot. "Really?"

White glowered at him and then said, "However, the tap on her cell phone has borne fruit in that regard." She retrieved a pocket digital recorder from her pants pocket and played it.

"Ami Pembleton."

"Ms. Pembleton? My name's Brandi Tagore, I'm with Clarion University?" The voice was obviously that of a student at the university, who had the tendency of the young to end their sentences as questions whether or not an interrogative was intended. "I'm the president of the Poli-Sci Club, and we've had a cancellation? See, we have a speaker, like, every month, and we were all set to have a reporter from the *Post,* but he had to cancel at the last minute. We need someone to give a talk on Saturday? You were on our list of people to invite for a future talk, actually."

"Um, Ms., uh—"

"Tagore."

"Right, Tagore—look, I'm flattered, but—"

"We'll, like, totally pay your way out here. There's a B and B you can stay at here in town—the Johnson House?—and we'll cover the travel, too. See, we usually do themes, ya know? This month the theme was political reporting, and we were gonna do lobbying in, like, two months, but—"

"Please, Ms. Tagore, if you could just give me a second?"

"I'm sorry, was I babbling? It's just that this is *such* an emergency and I'm *so* in trouble if I can't find a speaker, and—"

"Fine, I'll do it. I could use the break. Do you have my office number?"

"Yeah—I called there first, and your secretary gave me this number."

"Did she now? Well, call her back and arrange things with her."

"Oh, thank you *so* much, Ms. Pembleton! This is so great!"

White stopped the recording. While it was playing, Pink had sunk the five ball, but his attempt to sink the seven ball met with failure.

"Guess I need the stick after all," Orange said with a smile as she lined up a shot on the ten ball.

"So where's this Clarion University?" Bolan asked, though he already knew.

"Pennsylvania," White said. "Not far from Pittsburgh. The speaking engagement is in four days. Each of you is to make your way to Clarion. Fly, drive, take your pick—but do not tell me. The town is approximately 265 miles from here, and there are several hotels at the exit for the town on Interstate 80. Check into one. We shall meet again at the Denny's on Pennsylvania Route 68 near that exit on Thursday."

As Orange sank both the ten and the nine balls, Bolan said, "Want me to check out that B and B the college girl mentioned?"

"The hell *you* gonna do that for?" Pink asked snidely, though he was looking dolefully at the pool table as he said it, watching Orange sink the fourteen and fifteen balls with one shot.

Bolan smirked. "Marines didn't just teach me how to shoot stuff. I can scope out the joint, see if it'll present any opportunities for that clean termination the lady was talkin' 'bout."

White considered, then said, "Very well, Mr. Sapphire, you do that. Mr. Pink, your job will be to do the same for the university, with emphasis on the building where this Poli-Sci Club has its meetings."

Orange failed in her attempt to do a bank shot that would sink the twelve ball, so Bolan rechalked his cue stick as Pink said, "Why not just take her out on the road goin' up there?"

"Because according to a later conversation between Ms. Pembleton and her assistant, the university is putting her on an Amtrak train from Union Station to Pittsburgh," White said. "Then someone from the Poli-Sci Club will drive her to Clarion from there."

"Yeah," the Executioner said as he lined up a shot on the seven ball, "that's way too public."

"For you, maybe," Pink said. "Wouldn't be the first person I took down on a train."

"Mr. Sapphire is correct," White said. "There are too many variables on a moving train. Better that we strike when she is in a relatively remote location, away from her usual contacts."

"Not to mention," Orange said with a smile, "away from D.C."

Bolan sank the seven ball, then turned around and

sank the two ball and the six ball with one shot. Unfortunately, the cue ball then wound up between the eleven and twelve balls, all shots on the eight ball blocked. The Executioner tried to bank it off the side but missed the eight ball altogether.

That was a scratch, which meant that the women won the game without White ever touching her cue stick.

"Son of a *bitch*," Pink said. "Next game, I'm playin' with the old lady."

"There is no 'next game,'" White said tartly. "You have your assignments. We will meet again on Thursday."

Bolan said his goodbyes to the others, noting the scowl that Pink gave him, and departed.

So far everything was going smoothly. Barbara Price, who served as Stony Man's mission controller, had done an excellent impersonation of a college student on the phone, and Pembleton had jumped at the chance to get out of town for a weekend, which was predictable given her workaholic ways and busy schedule. The last variable had been convincing White to let Bolan be the one to check out the "Johnson House Bed and Breakfast," a nonexistent B and B on the outskirts of Clarion that was in reality an abandoned house scheduled for demolition that Stony Man was in the process of converting into a facsimile of an inn.

Since his assignment had been to watch the Pembleton-Brabson house, he had checked out of the airport hotel in D.C. and instead took his lodgings in a cheap motel not far from the bar. He walked back there intending to check out and then head to a rental car place for the 260-mile drive to Clarion.

When he got back to his room, he took out the sat

phone and dialed Stony Man. Once he was put through to Brognola, he simply said, "We're a go."

"Good work, Striker."

"Have you lined up the marshals, yet?"

"We've got a team of fifteen—five on three eight-hour shifts each. There'll be a CD with dossiers on each of them at the bed and breakfast when you get to Clarion."

"Good. Hope you have some backups."

"I've got twenty backups. I know how picky you are, Striker."

Again, Bolan said, "Good," and disconnected.

## 11

That evening, Bolan rented a small green Chevrolet Aveo, using the Michael Burns identity. It seemed like the wisest move, since nobody at the Black Cross besides Indigo could trace that name, and all he'd see was that he rented a car to do just what he was supposed to do for the Black Cross as "Mr. Sapphire."

He headed north on Interstate 83 to Harrisburg, then drove north on Route 22/322. The route would eventually take him to Interstate 80, and from there it'd be a straight shot to Clarion. By doing the drive late at night, there would be fewer cars on the road, and he'd be able to do what would normally be a five-and-a-half-hour drive in less than five hours.

Once he reached the town of Heckton, the road started to get dark, as there was just an open field on the right and the Susquehanna River on the left. Bolan knew from his earlier check of the maps of the area that there was a one-mile stretch of empty road with just nature on either side for a mile before he would reach the town of Dauphin.

There was only one other car on the road, but the Executioner was concerned, because the purple Ford Focus had been with him since he got off the interstate at Harrisburg. In all likelihood it was nothing—this was still a major thoroughfare—but Bolan had long since learned the importance of being aware of one's surroundings. Besides, one of the reasons he did a late-night drive was so that it would be more difficult for someone to follow him.

That concern grew when the Focus sped toward him without changing lanes.

Still driving with his left hand, Bolan's right went into his shoulder holster and, after unhooking the strap, he wrapped his hand around the grips of his .357 Desert Eagle and pulled it out of the holster.

The Focus rear-ended the Aveo—that was the driver's first mistake. The rear-ender always took more damage than the one being rear-ended, unless the former had a significant size advantage. The Focus had no such advantage on the Aveo; the Focus's driver served only to damage his own car.

Gunning the accelerator, the Focus driver then got into the left lane to pull alongside Bolan.

Sitting in the driver's seat was Mr. Pink, holding the steering wheel with his left hand and pointing a Para-Ordnance Nite-Tac .45ACP pistol right at Bolan, the flashlight attachment under the muzzle shining right in the Executioner's face. The passenger-side window was rolled down.

Pink yelled, "Pull over."

Bolan shook his head.

"I will shoot you in the *head* if you don't pull your ass over *right now*, Sapphire!"

Unwilling to roll down his own window, Bolan simply mouthed the words, *Go ahead.*

Snarling, Pink squeezed the trigger on the .45.

The Executioner had kept trying to get under Pink's skin because he hoped it would goad the man into making a mistake. That mistake turned out to be trying to fire a .45 one-handed.

The recoil sent Pink's right hand upward, causing the .45 round to slice into the Focus roof. At the same time, it also sent Pink sideways, but he maintained his grip on the steering wheel, forcing the car to swerve suddenly to the left—right into the K-rail dividing the road.

The body of the Focus squealed as it ground against the concrete of the K-rail. Pink struggled with the steering wheel, now gripping it with both hands, the Nite-Tac abandoned on the car floor.

Bolan pulled onto the shoulder of the road. He was more than happy to pull over, but on his terms, not Pink's. The last thing he wanted to do was to get into a shooting match while hurtling down a highway at fifty miles an hour, especially with a populated town less than a mile away.

Unlike the Stony Man vehicle he took to Valley Forge, the Aveo was *not* bulletproof, and Bolan still needed it to get to Clarion, so he moved away from it, holding the Desert Eagle with a double-handed grip.

Pink had regained control of the car and slammed on the brakes. The Focus's tires squealed, and the car whirled 270 degrees so the smashed-in front was now facing the K-rail, and the car was straddling both lanes. The next car to come up the road was going to slam right into it.

"Come out of the car slowly, Mr. Pink," Bolan said.

When there was no sign of movement, Bolan pulled

the trigger back, sending the .357 round sizzling through the air and ripping into the damaged body of the Focus.

As soon as Bolan saw movement, he dived to the pavement of the highway shoulder. Pink stuck his head out of the driver's window and—now gripping the .45 with *both* hands—shot back at Bolan. But he was firing blind, and the round whistled over the Executioner's head.

Pink ducked his head but started squirming out the window as he talked. "Don't be takin' this personal, Sapphire. It's just—well, you don't do nothin' that I already do, know what I'm sayin'? So you're expendable, and I'm just the man to expend you. 'Cause honestly? I really don't like you that much."

Bolan wasn't interested in talking. Taking aim at the spot on the Focus where he assumed Pink to be, Bolan fired several more rounds. The first two tore easily through the vehicle's body, and the third shattered both back windows, sending shards of glass all over the seat and the pavement. As more shots came, the car was starting to look like a piece of Swiss cheese.

If he hit Pink, there was no verbal indication from the man. He was enough of a professional that he might not have done so even if he was hit, so Bolan made no assumptions. Once he emptied the magazine, he ejected it, letting it fall to the pavement with a clatter. He reached into his jacket pocket and pulled out a fresh magazine, shoving it into the magazine with a loud click.

However, it turned out that Pink had also flattened himself on the pavement, and started shooting his Nite-Tac from *under* the car. The rounds richocheted off the pavement.

Bolan knew it was only a matter of time before Pink

adjusted his aim so that he'd hit the Executioner—
unless he moved.

So he crawled forward a bit, eventually rising to his
feet and squeezing off several more rounds. He wasn't
necessarily trying to hit anything, just laying down sup-
pression fire.

Running around to the other side of the Focus, he saw
that Pink had indeed been hit. As Bolan had predicted,
the man hadn't screamed, but at least one round from
the Desert Eagle had torn into Pink's left leg, pulverizing muscle and bone and the femoral artery, and left him
lying on the pavement, blood pouring onto the asphalt.
His dark skin had gotten somewhat pale, and sweat was
pouring down his face.

However, he was still holding up the Nite-Tac, and
he aimed it right at Bolan's face, the light shining in the
Executioner's eyes.

Refusing to let himself blink, Bolan had his Desert
Eagle aimed at Pink's head.

"Looks like we got us a Mexican standoff, Sapphire."

"That we do."

"What happened to your cracker accent?"

"You'll never know."

"Guess not."

"Why'd you come after me? We're supposed to be
on the same side."

"Wanted more money. Share's bigger with you dead,
and like I said, you ain't doin' nothin' I can't do."

"There's one thing I can do that you can't."

"What's that?"

"Live."

Pink actually laughed at that, but it degenerated into

a cough quickly. "You think you gettin' outta here alive, Sapphire?"

Even as Pink spoke, his Nite-Tac lowered a bit, the light no longer shining directly into Bolan's eyes. Again, he resisted the urge to blink; his eyes watered with the effort.

"I know I am," the Executioner said. "I hit you in your femoral artery. You'll bleed out in less than a minute."

Perhaps realizing that Bolan spoke the truth, Pink's finger tensed on the trigger.

That was the moment the Executioner had been waiting for. He fired the Desert Eagle. The .357 round screamed through the night air and shattered Pink's nose, skull and brain in rapid succession. Since Pink was lying on the ground, much of the damage exploded upward in a bloody mess. Pink's finger spasmed on the Nite-Tac's trigger, but the round fired harmlessly over Bolan's head, destined to land in the Susquehanna.

Amazingly, no cars had come up the road yet, though a few had gone south on the other side of the K-rail. They all slowed down to gape at what was happening, but nobody actually stopped, no doubt in part due to the large handguns both parties were carrying.

Bolan wasn't sure how long that would last, so he ran back to his car, while pulling the disposable cell phone the Black Cross had given him out of his pants pocket. He dialed 911 and then hit Talk.

"Nine-one-one operator."

"There's a car all messed up in the middle of the road on 22/322, just outside Dauphin," the Executioner said.

The operator started to ask another question, but Bolan hit End, dropped the disposable cell phone on the pavement and stepped on it. Then he got back into his

Aveo. He wasn't concerned about the shell casings from his Desert Eagle—the local police would never find a ballistics match. The Executioner's weapons were as off the grid as the man himself.

As he drove north on 22/322, continuing on his way toward Interstate 80, he said, "One down, six to go."

He still needed to find out who the other three assassins on Black Cross's payroll were, and he needed to execute White, Orange and Indigo.

But this was a good start.

**12**

There was a time when Brady's Bend, Pennsylvania, was a thriving limestone-mining town, but that time was long past. The three-mile-long town sat on one side of the Allegheny River, with East Brady on the other side. Any number of other industries had cropped up and crapped out in the area, and these days, the region's only real claim to fame was the fact that former Buffalo Bills quarterback Jim Kelly was born and raised in East Brady, something declared quite prominently on a large sign as you entered town after crossing the river.

The town's obscurity, combined with its remoteness made it an ideal place for a government safehouse.

After arriving in Clarion and checking into a Days Inn, one of the many hotels just off the Clarion exit on Interstate 80, Bolan drove his rented Aveo down Route 68 to Brady's Bend, turning off a small road that went up a steep hill. At the top of the hill was a long limestone-covered pathway that led up another hill to a small house.

Bolan saw why the place was so attractive as a safehouse. It was out of the way even within Brady's Bend and was located on top of a very steep hill that made it easy to secure and defend.

According to Brognola, the safehouse was used by the FBI, CIA and NSA, with the safehouse's upkeep handled by the DOD.

Brognola himself was waiting for Bolan at the top of the hill. "Good to see you, Striker."

"Getting here was harder than expected." Quickly, the Executioner filled Brognola in on Mr. Pink's abortive assassination attempt.

"You think you were made?" Brognola asked.

Bolan shook his head. "He didn't give any indication. In fact, he seemed genuinely surprised when I spoke to him without Mr. Sapphire's accent. No, this was motivated by pure greed and dislike. If anything, it simplifies the op—assuming the others believe me when I tell them what happened. Luckily, it'll have the ring of truth about it, seeing as how it actually happened."

"Hope so. Let's go inside. You can inspect the place, and I'll show you the dossiers on the marshals."

Brognola led Bolan into the small house, which on the outside looked like a simple cottage. There was only one entrance. It had a screen door that looked fairly standard, but upon closer inspection was reinforced with steel bars. It took an effort to open it. Behind that was a door made of wood on the outside, but also reinforced with steel.

As they walked in, a beeping sound started. Brognola walked over to a keypad and entered fourteen numbers, after which the beeping stopped.

"The password changes daily," Brognola said, "and is always between ten and twenty characters."

Bolan looked around. To the left was a small kitchen with very old-fashioned appliances. The Executioner suspected that the decor hadn't changed much since the cottage was first built.

To the right was a more modern-looking living room with a long couch, an easy chair and a rocking chair. There was a plasma-screen television with a DVD/VCR combo player attached, as well as a box that went to the satellite dish located atop the cottage, and a full stereo system with turntable, CD player, tape player and iPod deck. On the far end of the living room was a small desk with a laptop attached to a laser jet printer. A Webcam was mounted on top of the laptop monitor.

"Lose the satellite dish," Bolan said, "and whatever Internet connection the place has. These people have proved themselves to have excellent resources, and they might be able to piggyback a Net connection or a satellite signal."

Brognola simply nodded.

The cottage had just one bedroom, but only the person being protected would be sleeping here. There was a king-size bed, and a desk that had a legal pad and a cup full of pens and pencils. There was a television in this room, though it was a standard large-screen, with another DVD/VCR combo player and another satellite box.

Bolan also noted that the windows all around the house were wired and protected by vertical steel bars.

The bathroom was small, with a toilet, a pedestal sink and a shower stall.

Satisfied that the place was relatively secure, particularly once Brognola took care of the satellite dish, he said, "Let's see the marshals."

Sitting down at the living-room desk, Brognola

touched the button that would bring the laptop back from standby mode.

All thirty-five marshals—the fifteen first choices and twenty backups—were displayed on the screen.

"One second," Brognola said. "I need to have Bear check on something." He called up an e-mail program and sent a note to Kurtzman asking him to check into the incident on Route 22/322.

Once that was done, Bolan stood over Brognola, reading each dossier in turn. He approved of Brognola's first four choices, but not the fifth or sixth. "They both have spouses and children."

"So did two of the first four," Brognola pointed out.

"One was divorced, the other's kids were grown."

"All right." Brognola closed the windows containing those two.

The seventh was Clifford Minaya, someone Bolan recognized from a past operation. "He's a marshal now?"

Brognola nodded. "You know him?"

"We crossed paths a few years back, when he was Chicago PD. Almost ruined an operation with his bungling. Wasn't entirely his fault—he didn't know what was really going on—but I'd rather not trust him with this."

Brognola closed Minaya's folder and went to the next one, whom Bolan also recognized, but more favorably.

"Tanya Guthrie's the one who kept Olga Ousmanova safe from Petrov's people back in '02. I want her on the overnight."

"Why?"

"From what I've seen of the Black Cross, they take their opportunities at nonstandard times and places.

If they *do* find out about this safehouse and make a move on it, it'll be late at night. Guthrie's one of the best there is and I want her where she can do the most good."

Eventually, Bolan was able to settle on fifteen he thought were acceptable, before he had even gone through all twenty backups.

"They'll be on three eight-hour shifts, five per shift," Brognola said. "Two inside the house, three on the perimeter."

At first, Bolan thought there should be more inside the house, but then looking around, he realized that it was simply too small for that to be practical. The kitchen and living room were in the front of the house, separated only by the front door, but it was an open space between them with no wall, and the bedroom and bathroom in the back of the cottage was also a small area. One person in front and one in back would work, and the outdoors was sufficiently open and vast that a three-person perimeter was preferable.

Bolan then checked the grounds themselves. He was heartened to discover that there was simply no way to approach the house in daylight without being seen. The hill that one drove up to get to the house was an almost entirely open field with no cover to speak of. That was true of three of the four approaches to the house.

That left the fourth, which was behind the house. The hill continued up behind it, which was another open field—up to a point. Eventually, there was a tree line, and that was the source of Bolan's concern.

Climbing up the steep hill, with Brognola right behind him, Bolan inspected the tree line. The forest suddenly became very thick past the line, so the only viable spot for a sharpshooter would be right on the edge.

However, turning around, he saw that there was a clean shot at the house from the edge of the tree line.

Pointing at the ground, Bolan said, "We'll need Claymores all along here. This is the biggest hole in this location's security, and it's exactly the sort of thing the Black Cross will exploit."

Brognola blinked. "For a single sharpshooter? That's a little extreme, don't you think?"

"Normally, yes, but these people are too dangerous. Overkill is the only kind of kill that will work. Besides, it may be more than one sharpshooter."

"All right, we'll get them planted tonight."

"Good. That should do it, then. You'll take care of extracting Pembleton?"

Brognola nodded.

"Leave something with a heat signature in place."

"Of course," the big Fed stated.

"Good."

They went back to the house. Brognola noticed that there was a new e-mail from Stony Man.

"Interesting," Brognola said. "Your Mr. Pink had no ID on him, and they haven't gotten a print hit on him yet, either. But there's also no evidence of who shot him—no ballistics matches on the shells."

"Keep me posted. I'd like to know who it really was that I shot—and why he shot at me," Bolan said.

"Sure."

"I'd best head back to Clarion. We have our meet-up at Denny's tonight."

"Good luck, Striker. I'll handle things on this end."

With a final shake of Brognola's hand, the Executioner left the small cottage and headed to his rental car for his dinner date with the Black Cross.

**13**

Before she was Ms. Orange, she had been Martina White, and before that, she had been Martina Cassavettes.

It still confused the hell out of her when people called the Russian woman by her pseudonym, because she had been "Ms. White" since 1966, when she married Harold C. White.

Harold insisted on the "C," as if it made him important or something.

They had been high school sweethearts, Martina and Harold. He didn't want to go to college because that would keep him from being drafted, and Harold wanted to fight for his country. Martina wanted to go to college. Specifically, she wanted to go to Yale, but they didn't allow women. She had found that annoying.

Instead, she went to a small community college while Harold went off to join the Navy.

While on campus, she was raped by a fellow student, a physical education major named Gabe. She'd been wearing a miniskirt—all the girls were doing it, after all, it *was* 1967. She had tried to press charges, but Gabe was an upstanding young man. The police all thought she was asking for it, and the district attorney wasn't interested.

To make matters worse, she was pregnant. Since Harold hadn't been home for several months, it had to have been Gabe's baby. Unwilling to mother a child of the man who raped her, she found a doctor who was willing to break the law and give her an abortion.

Unfortunately, law-breaking doctors weren't always the most skilled. The procedure got rid of Gabe's child, but also damaged her uterus. She'd never be able to give birth.

When Harold came home for a furlough, Martina told him that it was a genetic thing, that several women in her family, including an aunt, a great-aunt, and two of her cousins, hadn't been able to have children, either.

She never told him about Gabe.

After the rape, Martina started taking self-defense classes at the college. That proved pointless. She had thought they were designed to help women protect themselves, but the instructor mostly just tried to show them how to use their purse as a weapon.

So Martina did her research and found a karate dojo. Not very many women took karate in those days, but there were two at the same dojo, which was taught by a Japanese-American man who pushed everybody equally hard.

The other two women washed out of the class after a year or so. Martina stuck with it.

She became one of the best students in the dojo and vowed that the next time some man tried to attack her, she'd be ready.

By the time she got her black belt, the kung-fu craze was going full bore, so Martina was able to open her own dojo. She specialized in teaching women, because it was still difficult for a female to be taken seriously as *karateka*. Thanks to the popularity of people like Bruce Lee, though, everyone wanted to at least try it.

Besides which, women who got assaulted by men still had a hard time getting police or prosecutors to give a damn.

Harold had come back safely from two tours in Vietnam, serving in the U.S. Navy overseas. When he returned home, they put together a down-payment on a house with his veterans' benefits.

Everything seemed to be going smoothly in their lives. The dojo was doing well, and Harold had a job at a local factory as a manager. Harold's job paid for the mortgage. The dojo didn't make much money, especially with the costs of renting the space and the upkeep, but it wasn't losing money, either.

One day, though, a pipe burst in the women's bathroom in the dojo. The water damage was minimal, and the plumber came and fixed things in fairly short order, but she had to close early that day.

She came home to find Harold in bed with another woman. They were both naked, in a position that Harold had never asked Martina to try.

Martina was furious. The woman was Jane, Harold's secretary at the factory. Harold's own office looked out over the factory floor, so he couldn't have sex with her in the office in the time-honored tradition of bosses everywhere. Instead, he took her home when he thought his wife should've been off doing that silly women's lib stuff at her little kung-fu place.

Martina broke Harold's neck.

It was, quite simply, the most wonderful sensation she'd ever felt in her life.

The feel of Harold's head and chin in her hands, the snap of bone as she twisted his head, the light going out of his eyes, his limp and lifeless body collapsing to the floor of their bedroom in a heap of useless limbs.

For the first time since she was raped, Martina was happy.

She let the secretary live. Jane promised Martina that she'd never tell anyone what happened. Martina promised Jane that, if she did, Martina would kill her, too. Jane—just an innocent girl who worshipped her big, strong Navy veteran boss—was quite frightened, and didn't want to do anything to risk her own life.

Martina then took Harold's body into the bathroom, dumped it in the tub, and ran the water of both the bath and the shower constantly while she cut his body apart, the running water washing the blood down the drain.

Once Harold's body was in sufficiently small pieces, she took each chunk and put it in the meat grinder, then, once the skin and bone and sinew and muscle was ground enough, dumped the contents down the drain.

She got through most of it before the blender burned out from the exertion.

The next day she called the police, saying her husband never came home from work the previous night. Jane played along, saying that she and Harold left early to investigate a new office site—the cover story the pair of them had given when they left the factory— but that he'd sent her back to the factory when they were done, saying he was going to surprise his wife at her kung-fu school.

But, Martina explained to the police, she closed the dojo early, and never saw Harold.

The police investigated and they, of course, found nothing.

Meanwhile, Martina had discovered something she enjoyed even more than Karate and Kung-fu.

She'd been keeping tabs on Gabe. He was now a coach at a local high school, where he no doubt went after the fresh meat attending classes there. In fact, it took only a little investigative work to discover that he'd raped three of the students under his care. None of them had been believed, and therefore none had been able to get anyone to press charges. Indeed, they'd been accused of conspiring to ruin the coach's good name.

Martina, though, recognized the pattern. Gabe hadn't changed a bit since college. She decided she needed to exact revenge on him the way she did on Harold.

They never found Gabe's body, either.

Since Harold hadn't actually been declared dead, Martina couldn't get his insurance benefits for another seven years, so she sold the house and rented a small apartment. She continued to run the dojo, but also took whatever opportunity she could to kill people who deserved it.

She progressed to killing people who may not have deserved it, but had wronged someone Martina cared about.

Then she started killing people because someone paid her to do so. Initially, Martina had used that money to help out the three girls Gabe had raped. But after a while, she just killed anyone she was paid to kill. And after a while, she kept the money for herself.

Once she started killing for money, it quickly became the only reason she killed—with one exception. Jane had fallen on hard times, having become addicted to heroin, and she had tried to give Martina up to get out of a drug charge.

By that time, Martina had enough money to hire the best lawyers, and there was no evidence, so nothing came of it and Jane was sentenced to rehab. Martina waited until she left the rehab center. Then she grabbed her and injected her with an impressive amount of heroin that Martina had purchased that morning on the street. Jane overdosed almost instantly, and Martina left her on the ground in an alley.

Just another junkie who had OD'd. Nobody would care about her, any more than they had cared about Martina when she'd been raped.

Her skills at leaving no evidence behind had attracted the Black Cross. In fact, she had been one of its founding members, and was the only one of the original members left. She even predated Mr. Indigo.

She had refused any number of promotions and had no interest in retiring. Hell, she'd made enough money to live a life of ease years before she joined the Black Cross.

No, she kept doing it because, even now in her sixties, nothing in the world gave her the same thrill as seeing, feeling, watching someone die at her hands.

Mostly because every time she killed someone, she imagined it was Gabe.

Or Harold.

Or Jane.

She sat now in the Denny's where they'd been told to meet on Pennsylvania Route 68, just off the interstate.

Ms. Orange had never liked these chain "family" restaurants. But she saw why Ms. White had chosen it. Nobody would look twice at them here.

Ms. White arrived a few minutes after Ms. Orange, wearing yet another outfit that accentuated her breasts. Then again, with breasts like those, it was pretty much impossible *not* to accentuate them unless she wore a burlap sack. She sat in the four-person booth across from Ms. Orange.

"Good to see you," Ms. Orange said companionably.

Ms. White, though, wasn't feeling companionable. "There is a job. We will do it."

"Somehow it just figures that the men are late."

"In more ways than one," a Southern-accented voice said from behind them.

Bolan approached them in Mr. Sapphire mode, looking furious.

"What do you mean?" Ms. White asked.

Taking a seat next to Ms. Orange, Bolan sounded as though he was barely keeping his temper in check and his volume down. He appeared to be very angry about *something*.

"You want the good news or the bad news?"

"We should wait for Mr. Pink," Ms. White said.

"No need for that," Bolan said, waving his hand back and forth. "Good news first, then—I scoped out the B and B, and it's remote. Ain't nothin' else around for half a block or so, and it'll be easy as apple pie to take the lady out without nobody bein' the wiser."

Tightly, angrily that Mr. Sapphire hadn't chosen to wait until Mr. Pink arrived to give his report, Ms. White asked, "And what is the bad news?"

"I'm drivin' up here, mindin' my own damn business, and Pinko decides to run me off the damn road!"

"What?" Ms. White and Ms. Orange both exclaimed simultaneously.

"That can't be," Ms. Orange said.

"Yeah, well, y'all mighta noticed he wasn't all that fond of me from jump. Last thing he told me 'fore I busted a cap in his head was that he wanted more money, and I didn't do nothin' he didn't do."

"What did you do with the body?" Ms. White asked.

"Left it there. The hell else was I supposed to do with it?"

"Are you insane?" Ms. White hissed. "He was one of us."

"Was he? All I saw was some nut job tryin' to run me off the road—the same someone that's been ridin' my ass since I started this gig. Look, *you* people recruited *me,* all right? I was just mindin' my business at a gun show when that Galloway feller came and gave me a card." He stared right at Ms. White. "And then *you* sent six men to clean my clock. Seems to me that y'all recognize the skills. So don't be givin' *me* what-for…."

This, to the Executioner, was the moment of truth. He hadn't wanted to jump the gun and kill Pink, but Pink himself had given him no other option. Since he had no interest in aiding the Black Cross in performing in secret, of *course* he was going to leave Pink's body on the empty road in central Pennsylvania, but he had to convince White and Orange that Sapphire's reasons for doing so were sound—since, by their standards, Bolan's reasons were most definitely not.

"Did you at least tell Mr. Indigo?" Ms. Orange asked.

"Hell no. Last thing he said was that we only talk to Whitey here. 'Sides, I dumped and broke the disposable cell phone, too, seein' as how it might be on Pink's phone. Y'all should do likewise."

"It has been two *days,*" Ms. White said angrily.

Bolan shrugged. "Ain't my fault. Y'all set this thing up. Anyhow, I ain't been idle for them two days. Wanna hear what I learned 'bout the B and B?"

Ms. White seethed for several seconds, and Ms. Orange feared she would strangle Mr. Sapphire right there in the family restaurant, but she got hold of herself. "Yes," she said in a tight voice.

"Place is in the middle of nowhere, out on Route 68. Ain't hardly nothin' 'round, 'cept for trees and stuff. No security, neither—front and back door have dinky little chain locks, and the people that run the place ain't there at night. I checked with them, makin' like I was a tourist who wasn't happy with my stay at the Holiday Inn, and wanted an alternative for next time I blew through town. They let loose that they only had one guest this weekend. I'm figurin' that's our girl, so after dark, she ought to be alone."

"Assuming no one checks in off the street in the meantime," Ms. Orange added.

The Executioner knew that wouldn't happen. "Yeah, assumin'. But we can take care of her right quick tomorrow night after she checks in and the owners head out."

"She'll be *completely* alone in the house?" Ms. White asked incredulously.

"That's not unusual," Ms. Orange said. "B and Bs

usually leave the guests to their own devices. It's like being a house guest."

Ms. White blew out a breath. "Very well. We will converge here tomorrow night at midnight, and then proceed to the Johnson House. We will kill Ms. Pembleton and erase any evidence."

"How you plannin' on doin' that?" Bolan asked. "'Cause I got me some notions that—"

Angrily, Ms. White said, "You will be told that after I have spoken to Mr. Indigo and we decide whether or not to let you live." She turned to Ms. Orange. "You are to accompany him to his hotel. He will check out. Then bring him to your hotel room. Under no circumstances are you to let him out of your sight."

"Aw shucks, darlin'," Bolan said with a grin, "can't *you* be my babysitter?"

Ms. Orange rolled her eyes. "Get your mind out of the gutter, young man."

"I'm just foolin', Gramma. I don't mind havin' someone with your moves watchin' my back."

"Her job," Ms. White said, "is to watch your *front,* Mr. Sapphire. And it's more than likely that, after I speak to Mr. Indigo, she will be instructed to break your fool neck. You have jeopardized *everything.*"

"I ain't jeopardized squat. Old Pinko rear-ended *me* and then started shootin'. The hell else was I *supposed* to do but whip out the old Desert Eagle and shoot back?"

Ms. Orange nudged him. "Come on, Mr. Sapphire, let's get you checked out."

"What, now? Ain't we gonna eat first?"

"We'll order room service at the hotel," Ms. Orange

said. "The food's bound to be better than the prepackaged crap in this place."

Bolan shrugged. "Fine, whatever. I just wanna get this job done so's I can get paid."

As Ms. Orange led him out of Denny's, Bolan was pleased. He wasn't sure what the Black Cross's resources were, but if they were able to learn what the evidence at the scene was, they'd soon be able to put together that the Focus had indeed rear-ended somebody—based on the smashed grille—and the shell casings left would be from a .357 Desert Eagle. Mr. Pink's own comments throughout the job would lend credence to Bolan's story.

He was only maintaining the story because he needed to fake Pembleton's death. Successful execution of the job would bring Mr. Sapphire deeper into the Black Cross's inner circle, allowing him to determine where their new headquarters would be and who the remaining three assassins were.

But if they didn't believe him, then he'd take Ms. Orange and Ms. White down and figure out another way in. No matter what happened, Pembleton would be the Black Cross's last contract.

**14**

Ms. White was furious as she spoke to Mr. Indigo on the secure cell phone the next day. "I thought you said he was vetted."

"He *was*. Thoroughly. And you were there when he was attacked in Valley Forge and took out a team of trained—"

"I don't mean Mr. Sapphire, you idiot," Ms. White said impatiently, "I mean Mr. Pink."

That brought Mr. Indigo up short. "What are you talking about?"

"Mr. Pink has spent most of this job attempting to undermine and threaten Mr. Sapphire. It is of no surprise to me that he would have done what Mr. Sapphire claims he did. Besides, I assume that the evidence backs him up, given that you *didn't* start this conversation with an order for me to terminate Mr. Sapphire?"

Cursing the woman's sharpness while simultaneously realizing that promoting her had been the right thing to do, Mr. Indigo said, "As far as we can tell, yes. The local cops got a witness statement from a truck driver who saw the car that Mr. Pink was driving rearend Mr. Sapphire's. The damage to the grille of Mr.

Pink's rental is also consistent with that. Given Mr. Sapphire's performance at Valley Forge, I'm not surprised that he got the upper hand, and all things considered, his actions were the right ones."

"As I suspected," Ms. White said with a sigh. "I am not pleased, but Mr. Pink obviously gave him little choice. So again, I have to ask, how thoroughly did you really vet Mr. Pink?"

"Does it matter?" Mr. Indigo said defensively. "He's dead, and there's nothing to tie him to us. He had a disposable phone just like the rest of you, and the only numbers on it are the other disposables. When they run his prints and DNA, they won't find anything."

That brought Ms. White up just as short. "I beg your pardon?"

"Mr. Pink didn't have a criminal record, or a military one. We'll be fine."

In fact, Mr. Pink—who was born LaMont Hawkins— had gained quite a reputation on the streets of East Los Angeles as an enforcer for drug crews, but he'd never been arrested. In fact, aside from one detective in the LAPD's Robbery-Homicide Division, a ten-year veteran named James Moreland, no one even suspected that Hawkins was the person responsible for so many drug murders.

Moreland was considered a lunatic loose cannon, and he was eventually drummed out of the LAPD because of what his superiors viewed as a "crusade" regarding LaMont Hawkins. In fact, many of the brass didn't think Hawkins really existed, though Moreland and others had brought him in for questioning once or twice. However, he was never fingerprinted or processed in any way, so he wasn't in the system. He never got a social security number, and never filed income tax by virtue of never having any on-the-books income. He had a driver's license, but that had been the only piece of paper on him.

As for Moreland, after being forced out of the police department, he drifted until he found himself recruited by an old man who called himself Mr. Violet. He was retiring from his position as the coordinator for the Black Cross, and he needed a replacement.

From that day forward, Moreland was known as Mr. Indigo, and his first action in his new job was to recruit LaMont Hawkins. He'd already proved himself to fit perfectly within the Black Cross's mandate.

Which was how Mr. Indigo could state with confidence that Mr. Pink's background was well-vetted. Detective Moreland had dedicated his career to trying to nail LaMont Hawkins, and had a string of failures and a premature pension to show for it. As a result, he knew Hawkins better than anyone.

Ironically, they had become respected colleagues, now that they were both on the same side. Hawkins much preferred the complex work that the Black Cross did, as the drug hits were starting to bore him. Besides, the drug lords he came up with were all doing time, and the new generation of dealers didn't understand the game the way they did back in the day.

Moreland had felt the same about the brass at the LAPD.

Unfortunately, Hawkins had always had a problem with white people. He almost never had to deal with them when he was LaMont Hawkins, and as Mr. Pink, he mostly just shot them. He'd had white colleagues in the Black Cross, of course, but there had never been a problem.

But then, none of them had been as aggressively good-old-boy as Mr. Sapphire.

"What about the job?" Ms. White asked, startling Mr. Indigo out of his reverie. "Will you send a replacement?"

"Do you think one is needed?"

"Unlikely." Ms. White had done some reconnaissance of her own of the Johnson House Bed and Breakfast, and her own observations matched those of Mr. Sapphire. "The three of us should be able to complete the job with ease."

"Good. I'll have Mr. Silver and Mr. Chartreuse standing by with the Black Hawk tonight."

"Late tonight," Ms. White said. "We will be making our move sometime after midnight, to make sure that the target is asleep."

"Roger that. Anything else?"

Ms. White smiled. "Yes. I expect my portion of Mr. Pink's share to be in my account by morning, Mr. Indigo."

With that, Ms. White hung up.

She almost threw the cell phone across the hotel room, but those phones weren't cheap. Of course, she could have done it with the disposable—she'd obtained new ones for herself, Ms. Orange and Mr. Sapphire—but then she'd just have to get another.

Her ideal form of relieving tension would be to seduce a young man and kill him while climaxing, but she preferred not to do that in the same jurisdiction as her Black Cross murders. Two unsolvable murders that close to each other was the kind of pattern that a canny law-enforcement officer might notice. True, the likelihood of finding such a creature in the middle of nowhere in Pennsylvania was remote, but it was better not to find out the hard way that the Clarion County Sheriff's Office had a budding Sherlock Holmes in its midst.

Instead, she stripped out of her sweater and jeans and took a long hot shower. It wasn't ideal—even the massage setting on the hotel shower and the scalding hot water couldn't pound all the tension out of her muscles—but the feel of the cascading hot water did relax her somewhat. Enough that she wasn't likely to explode and kill the first person who crossed her path. Besides, that person would likely be an innocent by-stander—a fellow hotel guest or a member of the cleaning staff—and Ms. White preferred to avoid killing innocent bystanders where at all possible.

At least, ones she wasn't having sex with.

She meticulously toweled herself dry, then she decided that she'd have a little bit of fun. She wore as skimpy a lace bra as she could get away with, then put on a skintight V-neck top that displayed her generous cleavage. She left the room and walked the long way to the hotel where Ms. Orange and, now, Mr. Sapphire were staying, watching as she got eye-goggling looks from the college boys.

It was a start, anyhow.

Going up to the room, she knocked and Mr. Sapphire opened the door. To her surprise—and disappoint-ment—his eyes didn't go directly to her chest. Instead, he stared her right in the eyes and asked, "Well? Am I out of protective custody or what?"

"I would prefer that you both remain here. The target will be checking in tonight, after all, and once the job is completed we will be evac'd to the new headquarters."

That was the best news Bolan had heard all day. It was therefore with genuine relief that he said in Mr. Sapphire's antebellum tones, "Glory hallelujah. So what time do we do the deed?"

"After midnight would be best."

"Great," the Executioner said. "That'll work out just fine."

THAT NIGHT, Ms. White, Mr. Orange and the Executioner in his role as Mr. Sapphire drove in Ms. White's rental SUV down Route 68, then veered off to the grass fields on the side of the road. According to the property records that Ms. Orange had obtained, the Johnson House owned this entire field.

Those online records had, of course, been manufactured by Aaron Kurtzman.

Bolan had both his Desert Eagle and SIG-Sauer. He left the rifle behind, since he was unlikely to need it. Indeed, if all went to plan, he wouldn't need either of the handguns, but it was best to be sure. He had backup ammo for both.

The SUV came to a halt about a quarter mile from the B an B. Ms. White had the same Charter Police Undercover .38 she'd used at Mohonk, as well as the late Mr. Green's 9 mm OD Green Glock 19. She'd scavenged it from Mr. Green's corpse when she—along with Mr. Silver and Mr. Chartreuse—had cleaned up the scene of Albert Bethke's assassination.

For her part, Ms. Orange had a .45 ACP Kimber Ultra Refined Carry Pistol II. Ms. Orange preferred the RCPs, as they were easy to place on your person and were less intrusive than larger pistols. Unlike her col-

leagues, she never bothered carrying a backup piece—
her contingency plan was always her martial arts skills
combined with her little-old-lady affect. However, she
did keep a couple of throwing knives around. Ms. White
had been kind enough to give her a couple of Mr.
Mauve's old Hibben UC-458s. She also had a Beshara
in her belt and a quartet of *shuriken* in her cardigan
pocket for emergencies.

Ms. White said, "Remain here" when they got within
sight of the B and B. She placed on her head a pair of
ATN PS-23-CGT night-vision goggles.

The Executioner had anticipated that she would have
such equipment, and had accounted for it in his plan.

Moving stealthily, Ms. White searched all around
the house, looking for heat signatures through the
goggles. The first floor was almost completely cold,
aside from the dim flash of green at about waist
height—likely the B and B's credit-card reader. There
was also a couple of very dim lights in the kitchen area
that likely corresponded to coffeemakers, microwaves
and digital clocks. One big, rectangular heat source was
probably the refrigerator.

Craning her neck upward, Ms. White scoped out the
upstairs, detecting only a tiny green light near the base-
board of one wall—probably a nightlight—and a
human-size heat source in one corner.

She went back to where her fellow assassins were
waiting. "Our recon was correct. There is only one
person in the building. I suggest we deploy in—"

Bolan held up a hand. "No need for that, Whitey," he
said with what had rapidly become a trademark grin of
Mr. Sapphire's. The Executioner hoped this would be

over soon—as the Sapphire-Burns persona was becoming quite wearing.

"No need for what?" Ms. White asked frostily.

Reaching into his jacket pocket with the hand that wasn't holding the Desert Eagle, Bolan took out a disposable phone. "These things are real handy, ya know? Not only can you make phone calls without nobody knowin' who owns the account, but you can use 'em as a detonator."

Ms. Orange blanched. "Detonator for what?"

"You see, folks, I wasn't just doin' recon when I scoped out the joint. I left a few gifts behind." He flipped open the disposable cell phone, dialed a number, then hit Send.

The Johnson House Bed and Breakfast exploded in a fiery conflagration of wood, steel, cloth, wiring and electronics and so much more. The deafening explosion echoed across the empty road of Route 68.

**15**

Both Ms. Orange and Ms. White, standing on either side of the Executioner, immediately whipped out their weapons. As soon as they reached for their guns, Bolan unholstered his Desert Eagle.

He found himself facing the muzzles of a Glock and an RCP II .45, Ms. Orange having shifted her position so that she and Ms. White were at forty-five-degree angles to Bolan. It was a small thing, but it bespoke Ms. Orange's professionalism. Where they were originally standing, Bolan could simply duck and the two women would shoot each other.

Since she was the more dangerous of the two—though only in relative terms—the Executioner had his own weapon pointed at Ms. White.

Behind them, the roar of the fire started by the explosion filled the previously quiet night air, and the light from the flames cast flickering shadows on all three of them. The fire's hungry maw gobbled up much of the oxygen and warped the air patterns, causing the hair of all three of them to ruffle and be blown about.

"The hell's the problem?" Bolan asked. "Thought the job was to kill the lobbyist lady and leave nobody none for the wiser. I just did that—and, I might add, all by my lonesome."

"We work as a *team,* Mr. Sapphire," Ms. White said tightly, "and plans for execution of jobs is also done as a *team.* You bypassed the chain of command."

"Yeah, well, I didn't have much use for that chain-of-command crap when I was a Marine, neither. 'Sides which, I figured that horse already left the barn when Pinko tried to ventilate me on Route 22."

In her grandmotherly voice, Ms. Orange said, "Put the pistol down, please, Mr. Sapphire."

"I ain't puttin' squat down till y'all do. That .45's a nice piece and all, but unless you get a perfect shot, I ain't goin' down from it right away, and my hand cannon here'll blow Whitey's head clear off."

Ms. White smiled, though it was more like an animal baring her teeth. "If you truly believe that you can blow my head clear off, as you so eloquently put it, before I pulverize your brain matter with one shot from this weapon, Mr. Sapphire, you are sorely mistaken."

"Look, the job's done, so what the *hell's* the problem? Grandma here scoped out the restaurant so we knew when the lobbyist lady was gonna be there, you did the cell-phone-shuffle thing, and that led us here, where I administered what my old sergeant used to call the coup de grâce. Sounds like teamwork to me, don't it?"

Bolan watched Ms. White's face closely. The woman had the look of a stone-cold killer, an expression the Executioner had seen on many a face. Her face showed absolutely no indication of what was going through her mind. She simply stared impassively at Bolan. While the Executioner knew that she was weighing the options, he could not say in what direction those thoughts were turning.

Eventually, though, she lowered the gun. Bolan did likewise. The entire setup he'd so carefully constructed would be for naught if they didn't now return to whatever the Black Cross's new headquarters were.

"What about that explosion?" Ms. Orange asked. "When they investigate—"

Bolan interrupted. "They ain't gonna find nothin'. Ain't no way they're gonna trace the C-4 I used, trust me."

Ms. White whirled, and for the first time Bolan noticed her expression change in a noncalculated manner. "Where did you get your hands on C-4?"

Grinning, Bolan said, "I got friends in low places, darlin'. Don't worry, ain't nobody gonna trace nothin' to me, and they ain't gonna trace it to y'all."

"I hope not, Mr. Sapphire, because if they do, you will find yourself very much alone in this."

"That's how the teamwork is, huh?"

Ms. Orange cut off Ms. White before she could reply. "We should table this discussion." As she spoke, the distant sound of sirens could be heard—and were growing closer by the second.

"Agreed," Ms. White said. "We'll proceed to the rendezvous point and signal our evac from there."

They proceeded in silence to the SUV. Ms. White drove the vehicle off-road for a bit longer, coming out on a side street that emptied onto Route 68 much farther from the Johnson House. By the time they passed the site of the Johnson House, fire trucks were already trying to get the blaze under control, and deputies from the county sheriff's office were redirecting traffic.

Ms. White rolled down her window and put on a surprisingly good Southern accent. "What's goin' on, Officer?"

The deputy had a stone-faced expression. "We got us a fire, ma'am. Just keep movin' on, please, we need to keep the area clear."

"Was anybody hurt?"

"We are unclear on that at the moment, but there may have been one person in the house at the time."

"Such a pity. Hope y'all get it under control."

"Thank you, ma'am, now please, if you'd move along."

"Course, Officer."

With that, Ms. White rolled the window back up and drove back down Route 68.

Back in her Russian-accented speaking voice, Ms. White said as she drove, "We will leave the SUV in a field on the other side of town, and I will signal the evac chopper."

"You're just gonna leave the SUV?" Bolan asked.

"The name and credit card it was registered under are quite false and completely untraceable."

The Executioner had figured as much, but it was best to be sure. "So was my Aveo—name on the credit card's one of my buddies who died in the desert." In truth, it was rented under the name of Michael Burns—a false name—but Ms. White and Ms. Orange couldn't know that without risking Bolan's cover. "So I guess leavin' it in Grandma's hotel parkin' lot's okay?"

"Of course."

After driving all the way through Clarion, they went a bit farther on Route 68, which turned into Miola Road once they got out of town. They continued north until they were driving alongside a wide open field. Ms. White drove the SUV into the field, then took out her disposable cell phone and pressed the number 5.

"The chopper will be here soon. They will take us to headquarters, after which, Mr. Sapphire, you and I and Mr. Indigo will have a discussion about protocol."

"Always happy to have a discussion," Bolan said gamely.

What mattered was that he was headed to the new Black Cross headquarters.

Within a few minutes, the Executioner heard the sound of copter blades grow close. Looking upward, he saw a dark green UH-60L Black Hawk helicopter on approach.

A rope ladder lowered from the Black Hawk. The short, squat form of Mr. Chartreuse, the Black Cross's evac chief, climbed down the rope ladder. Once he was most of the way down, he hopped off the ladder, landing on the ground with a semisolid thump of boot on mud.

"Everything taken care of?" he asked.

"Yes," Ms. White said. Glaring at Bolan, she said, "No cleanup is necessary."

"How'd you swing that?"

Letting loose with one of Sapphire's grins, the Executioner said, "C-4 is your friend—well, leastaways, it's mine."

Mr. Chartreuse shrugged. "Whatever works. Let's go."

ALLEN BRADLEE HAD JUST finished his Reuben sandwich when his cell phone rang. The words Blocked Caller ID were on the display. Activating the phone, he put it to his ear and said, "Allen Bradlee."

The voice of Mr. Indigo sounded on the other end. "The job is complete, Mr. Bradlee."

"Really?" Bradlee hadn't heard any news reports of a lobbyist dying. "When? Where?"

"The event occurred in Clarion, Pennsylvania. It might be some time before the specifics are revealed to the public due to the rather explosive nature of the event."

Bradlee nodded. He had to admit that he hadn't been expecting them to take her out with something so crude as an explosion, but he wasn't about to look a gift horse in the mouth. The police probably hadn't been able to identify the body yet, if it was a bomb of some kind. As long as Ami Pembleton was dead, it almost didn't matter how.

Then he finally registered the location. "She was in Clarion?"

"A speaking engagement at the local college's political science club. It provided a better opportunity than the middle of D.C."

"All right. Thank you, Mr. Indigo. The remainder of the fee will be transferred shortly."

"Good to know."

Bradlee ended the call. Something was bothering him, but he wasn't sure what. He kept reading the same paragraph of the same op-ed piece in the *Post* before he finally gave up, folded up the paper and went to his car to head back to Fort Meade.

As he drove north on the Baltimore-Washington Parkway, it finally occurred to him what was bothering him.

He arrived back at the office and, rather than effect the transfer, as he'd promised, he instead called up the day's e-mail. It was a memo he'd been CC'd on, something about a safehouse....

Yes, there it was. A request from the FBI to use a safehouse in Brady's Bend, only a few miles from Clarion, Pennsylvania. Said request was turned down, but there were no specifics, and no indication of what agency had use of it, only that the safehouse had been tagged as unusable going back a couple of days, with no timetable for when it would be available again.

Bradlee's entire job was determining patterns, and this one didn't look right to him.

The first thing he did was call Clarion University's political science department, and asked if the student club was having a lobbyist named Ami Pembleton as a speaker.

They were not.

The second thing he did was to try to track down who was using the Brady's Bend safehouse. It was eyesonly above Bradlee's own clearance. Very few things were above Bradlee's clearance, which meant the blackest of black ops.

The third thing he did was track down any explosions that might have happened in Clarion, Pennsylvania. By this time, the day was almost over, as Bradlee had done the scut work all by himself, telling Glynis to hold any calls. Normally, Glynis did the tedious jobs for him, but if he got her involved in this, Spencer would blow a gasket.

Eventually, though, Bradlee figured it out, and determined that there was an explosion at the Johnson House Bed and Breakfast in Clarion. According to the owners, there was only one guest, but that guest had not been identified yet.

The fourth thing he did was search for records of the

Johnson House B and B. He found very little indication that the place existed before a week earlier.

The fifth thing he did was call Higby's Imports and Exports. Bradlee wasn't completely certain, but given the importance of this job and how much they'd paid for it, he needed to make sure the job was *truly* finished—and the Black Cross wasn't getting the rest of its fee until Bradlee was sure it was.

## 16

After arriving at the new Black Cross HQ—located in a remote location in Chippewa County, Michigan, not far from Sault Ste. Marie—White, Orange and the Executioner were thoroughly debriefed, and then escorted to bunks where they could get a good night's sleep.

The next morning, Bolan woke up, showered and shaved, dressed in a simple black T-shirt and blue jeans, and then reported to Indigo, as he had been told to do the night before.

Also present were Orange, this time wearing a beige turtleneck and white Capri pants; White, wearing a one-piece navy blue jumpsuit that zippered up the front and was about a size too small for her, hugging her curvy form; that hyperactive kid at the laptop and a man he'd never met. He was very tall, with a shaved head and a long chin beard that extended almost to his clavicle. His skin tone marked him as being from the Middle East.

Indigo introduced him as Mr. Blue.

"We got us a new job?" Bolan asked.

Sounding quite angry, Indigo said, "Not exactly. Turns out the old one may not be finished yet, Mr. Sapphire."

"What's with the evil eye at me?" Bolan asked, wondering how the op had been compromised.

"Our client has reason to believe that the target wasn't present at the B and B when you blew it up. Our client also thinks that the B and B in question may have been a fake."

"That's nuts!" Even as Bolan expressed Mr. Sapphire's annoyance, his own mind was turning over the problem. Whoever hired the Black Cross had impressive resources in addition to the deep pockets they'd needed to hire them in the first place.

Orange, thankfully, came to his rescue. "I checked the Johnson House's property records. It looked clean to me."

"Maybe, maybe not. The remains in the fire haven't been identified yet, but our client also noticed that a government safehouse near Clarion's been taken over by some black ops group or other. They don't know by who, but the timing and the proximity has the client nervous. Therefore we're to investigate this safehouse, and if the target is alive and well and being hidden there, then we finish the job once and for all."

Red flags went off in the Executioner's mind. Whoever hired the Black Cross had very high-level access. Given who Pembleton had been pissing off lately, Bolan knew that wasn't a complete surprise, but the number of people who were privy to safehouse information of any kind was limited.

He needed a way to communicate this to Brognola and to get Pembleton moved.

Sadly, that wasn't going to happen, as Indigo went on, "You leave immediately. We've been given the specifics of the safehouse. Mr. Blue will provide you with the game plan en route."

Angrily, White asked, "Why him?"

"Because right now I'm not feeling particularly trusting toward any of the three of you," Indigo snapped. "This is an operation in which important intel was botched, one of our people was killed over something outside the job and the target may not have even been eliminated. It was sloppy work, and I hold all three of you responsible. Now go, get ready. Mr. Blue, you stay behind."

Bolan departed, not believing for a second that he wasn't the primary source of concern. He fully expected that his "fellow" assassins would turn on him in an instant. He'd be ready when that happened.

After the trio left, Mr. Blue turned to Mr. Indigo and said, "You really do not trust *any* of them?"

Shaking his head, Mr. Indigo said, "I know what you're thinking—Mr. Sapphire's the newest recruit, and he's the one who killed Mr. Pink. But none of them covered themselves in glory here. Not only that, but Galloway was the one who found Mr. Sapphire. He's never let us down before. And Ms. Orange was the one who didn't catch the problems in the B and B's background." Mr. Indigo sighed. "As for Ms. White, this was her first time running an op. She may have cracked under the pressure. Ms. Orange is getting old and Mr. Sapphire's still fitting in. If Pembleton really was secreted to a safehouse and there was someone else in the B and B, then we've got a leak somewhere. It could be any one of those three, or none of them. Your job, Mr. Blue, is to find out which of them it is, if any, and take care of him or her—or them."

Mr. Blue nodded. "Absolutely."

"In the meantime, I need to talk to Galloway. Our

ranks are getting dangerously thin, and I have the feeling that this job is only going to exacerbate that problem." Mr. Indigo sighed again. Heavy turnover due to either retirement or attrition was a common factor in running the Black Cross. Right now they were down to these four, plus Mr. Gray and Mr. Black.

Walking over to the printer attached to the laptop, Mr. Indigo removed the sheet that had just printed. "Here's the layout of the safehouse, according to the client."

After taking it, Mr. Blue departed, retreating to the barracks he'd been given. He pulled out his footlocker and tried to decide which weapon to bring with him. It was always difficult for him to narrow it down to two weapons, but it was also pointless to bring more than two. In all his years as a paid assassin, and prior to that as a member of the Republican Guard, he'd never needed more than two weapons for a fight. He doubted he'd need more this time, either.

He looked over the printout Mr. Indigo had given him. A house on a hill with open air on three sides and a steep hill going upward on the fourth side.

Given the terrain of the location, the best mode of attack would be from up the hill looking down on the safehouse, since whoever was guarding the place would have perfect line of sight in every other direction. So the first thing he packed was the Sabre Defence Industries 5.56 mm Signature Elite Massad Ayoob rifle that he'd had sandbagged years back. It hadn't been a sniper rifle before the sandbagging, but it was an excellent one now.

For anything that might be happening closer in, he brought along the Patriot Ordnance Factory P-415 .223. A bit extreme for taking on what was likely only a federal marshal or two guarding a safehouse, but the indication was that this might be a black ops deal, so he wanted to make sure he engaged in overkill.

Back when Mr. Blue was called Ahmed ibn Haroun al-Rashan, he learned quickly that overkill was best in these situations. He'd confronted paid CIA assassins and terrorist lunatics from every country in the Middle East and the armed forces of dozens of NATO countries. One high-caliber bullet *might* kill someone. Dozens of high-caliber bullets fired in rapid succession *definitely* killed someone.

However, al-Rashan found the fanaticism depressing. When you lived in the desert, you either chose a side or you died. And often when you chose a side, you still died. The desert sand never tired of absorbing blood, it seemed. After a while, al-Rashan grew weary of the attempts to disguise greed with politics and religion. The hypocrisy disgusted him. Yes, they claimed to believe in God, and were working for His greater glory. Yes, they claimed to be loyal to their leader, whoever that might happen to be this week. But mostly, they were loyal to cash and oil and the power that came with both those things.

After a time, al-Rashan wanted to simply stick with the greed. He was willing to admit that he didn't give a camel's ass for God or anyone or any idealism. He just wanted a great deal of money. He knew there was no afterlife, and there were no virgins waiting for him when he died. All that awaited him were vultures picking at his corpse. He'd accepted that long ago.

In the Black Cross, he'd found the perfect place. Away from the desert and its insatiable thirst for the blood of life, al-Rashan was able to put his skills as a sniper to a more fitting use.

After packing away both the P-415 and the Elite Ayoob rifles, he reported to the chopper pad. Or, rather, to the clearing outside the cabin where the dark green UH-60L Black Hawk had been placed, since there wasn't a proper pad here. Mr. Blue understood the need for security that prompted the Black Cross to change its headquarters regularly, but there were times when he wished they maintained proper facilities.

By the time he arrived, he already had a battle plan in place.

Everyone was already in the Black Hawk: Mr. Silver in the pilot's seat, Mr. Chartreuse next to him, and Ms. White, Mr. Sapphire and Ms. Orange in the bench-style seats in the rear compartment. "Let's go," he said as he climbed on board.

The Black Hawk took off. Mr. Blue put on a set of headphones and placed the mouthpiece by his lips. "Can everyone hear me?"

All three assassins nodded.

"Good. Here's the plan." He held up the printout with the safehouse's layout. "I will set up with a sniper rifle at the tree line at the top of the hill. Whatever assets are outdoors, I will take care of. Once that's done, the three of you will attack the safehouse itself and kill the target and anyone else inside."

"You think this will work?" Ms. White asked, sounding skeptical.

"The house is very small, and much of the occupants' time would be spent alone doing nothing. I suspect that most of the assets will be out of doors during the day, which is when we'll be attacking."

Bolan kept his poker face, but silently cursed. He'd

deliberately allocated the marshals in such a way that the best of them would be on the overnight shift.

"You that good a sniper?" Bolan asked, expecting that the man would be professional enough to answer at least semitruthfully.

"Yes." Mr. Blue spoke plainly. "Or so the Republican Guard thought when they had me perform such tasks against United States armed forces. Is that a problem, Mr. Sapphire?"

"No skin off my ass, Blue Boy. Hell, I just hope one of the guys you tagged was my old sergeant."

It took several hours—probably extending the absolute limit of the Black Hawk's fuel supply—to bring them to western Pennsylvania. Bolan recognized the terrain from when he'd studied the maps of the area prior to driving to Clarion, and soon enough recognized the area of Brady's Bend, just off the Allegheny River. The Black Hawk landed in a clearing about half a mile from the tree line where the Executioner had told Brognola to place the Claymores.

From the front, Mr. Silver said, "I'm gonna go refuel this puppy, so don't get it all done for another hour or so, okay?"

Ms. Orange smiled sweetly. "We'll do our best."

Once the Black Hawk took off, the four of them hiked in silence uphill and through the woods before reaching the appropriate spot.

Bolan deliberately hung back near an oak tree while Blue set up his Sabre. The Executioner wasn't sure exactly *where* the Claymores had been placed.

Unfortunately, Ms. Orange was doing likewise, trying to stay out of sight of the house from the bottom of the hill. Ms. White, though, had actually moved past Mr. Blue, which was tactically unsound.

In fact, Ms. Orange said as much. "What're you doing?"

"It is unlikely they are looking in this precise direction at this precise moment," Ms. White said as she removed a pair of binoculars.

Mr. Blue went through the entire process of assembling his weapon, finally placing an Optical Systems Technologies AN/PVS-22 night-vision scope—which was redundant on this bright sunny day—atop it before dropping to his belly and setting up his shot.

While doing so, Mr. Blue's elbow pressed against an M-5 Pressure Release Firing Device that was embedded in the dirt. As soon as his elbow moved again, thus releasing the pressure, it set off an M-18 A1 Claymore. A thin layer of C-4 detonated, projecting seven hundred steel balls into the air toward them.

Bolan winced as some of the mine's contents sliced through his left arm. It was only a surface graze, but it still tore through his flesh and the pain from it burned.

Mr. Blue wasn't so fortunate. The mine's payload plowed into his flesh, pulverizing bone and muscle instantly, and ripping through to the other side with little difficulty, leaving a shattered, bloody, smoking ruin of a corpse atop the now-empty Claymore mine.

Like Bolan, Ms. Orange had been near a tree, and had also been right behind Mr. Blue when he was ventilated. While the balls easily penetrated his body, their momentum was sufficiently retarded by passage through his body that by the time they reached her, they were less harmful. She also was lucky enough to have been far enough away to be under the mine's arc and had the wherewithal to dive to the dirt behind the tree at the sound of the explosion.

As a result, she had a severely bruised left side and left arm, both of which were pummelled by the lower-riding steel balls. The rest sailed over her head, embedding themselves in the dirt behind her.

Ms. White was the luckiest of all of them, as she had been in front of him, so while the force of the C-4's explosion propelled her to the ground, she was unhurt.

Unholstering his Desert Eagle, Bolan grabbed the stock with both hands and aimed it right at Ms. White's head.

Unfortunately, his wounded arm threw off his aim, and the .357 round whizzed over her head.

Ms. White did not give him a second chance to fire, as she squeezed off several shots from her 9 mm Glock, forcing Bolan to remain behind the cover of the oak.

When the firing stopped, he held up his Desert Eagle—only to find that Ms. White was nowhere to be seen. Stepping out from behind the tree, he saw that she was running down the hill.

He took aim and attempted to fire, when out of the corner of his eye, he noticed movement.

Even with the fair warning, he was barely able to roll with the jumping side kick that Ms. Orange hit him with. Had he remained where he was, she would likely have broken a rib or two. As it was, they both fell to the ground in a heap, and Bolan felt the fiery sensation of the impact of her hiking boot on his chest. Nothing was broken, but he'd have an impressive bruise come evening.

Both of them got to their feet at the same time. Again, Bolan raised his Desert Eagle, but Ms. Orange's left leg came up with a lightning-fast inside-out crescent kick. The side of her boot caught the Executioner on the wrist, forcing him to drop the weapon.

Not giving him a chance to recover, or even think, Ms. Orange used the momentum of her crescent kick to whirl and deliver a spinning back kick to Bolan's solar plexus. At the impact of her boot heel, the wind escaped from the soldier's body with a mighty whoosh as he stumbled backward, stooped over.

Ms. Orange whirled again, placing her hands on Bolan's shoulders—easy enough to do with him stooped over—and lifted her right leg so her knee collided with Bolan's jaw, sending his teeth rattling into one another.

As the salty taste of blood filled his mouth, Bolan thrust out a punch to Ms. Orange's stomach, not expecting it to actually hurt her, but to get her away from him for just a second so he could get his bearings. That was a good thing, as she had reared her right hand back to strike him with her palm heel, and there was every chance she'd hit his nose, shattering the bones within and sending them lodging into his brain, killing him instantly.

Any danger of underestimating Ms. Orange due to her age was out the window. Bolan had only faced one person who could kick as fast and effectively as Ms. Orange, and he was one-third of her age, and had been training since he was four years old.

The two of them circled each other, taking each other's measure. Both had their hands up, and both were waiting for the other to make a move. The Executioner dared not reach for his SIG-Sauer, as those precious seconds would enable Ms. Orange to strike once again.

For now, it would have to be hand-to-hand.

Bolan's only issue with that was how long it would take. He had to hope that the marshals he and Brognola had picked would be able to handle Ms. White.

The Executioner let loose with a couple of left jabs intended to force Ms. Orange to keep her distance. It would also make her think him to be a simple pugilist, a trained Marine but no more than that. He even made sure to move like a boxer, dancing around a lot.

In response, Ms. Orange let loose with a knife-hand strike to the temple that the Executioner easily blocked, but she followed it with a short punch to the ribs, then a punch up at his jaw.

That last punch he caught. He grabbed her wrist and flipped her over. For all her strength, she didn't weigh *that* much, and she whirled in the air and landed on her back with a thump.

Again, however, he underestimated her leg speed. Even as he lifted his leg to deliver a heel kick to her head, her legs popped up, the cuffs of the Capri pants enveloping his neck on both sides, then flipped *him* over with a scissor motion. Having been on the receiving end of such more than once, Bolan was able to relax his neck muscles enough that the action wasn't fatal, but it still wrenched his neck and put him on his back right next to her.

They both got to their feet and faced each other again. "Not bad," Bolan said, no longer bothering with Mr. Sapphire's accent.

"So it was you the whole time? I suppose you went after Mr. Pink, too."

Bolan said nothing. Saying "not bad" was a stalling tactic to allow him to catch his breath, but he had it now and wasn't about to waste anymore energy talking.

Besides, his answer didn't matter. Only one of them was walking away from this confrontation alive. If it was Ms. Orange, her knowing the truth would be of no interest, because Bolan would be dead. If it was Bolan, the knowledge would do Ms. Orange even less good.

The pain from the wound in his arm was starting to burn fiercely, but Bolan had suffered far worse in his time. His main concern was the blood loss. The longer this fight went on, the weaker he would get. He needed to finish off Ms. Orange so he could bind the wound and stanch the blood flow.

Deciding it might be worth the risk, he reached under his jacket for the SIG-Sauer.

As he did so, another lightning-fast crescent kick caught Bolan on the temple. His head swam, his vision swirling from the impact. She followed it with a punch to the face that sent him stumbling backward.

But he still had his hand on the SIG-Sauer. Stumbling back even farther than the punch had sent him, he got just enough distance so he could whip out the handgun and squeeze the trigger.

One bullet ripped through Ms. Orange's beige turtle-neck and splintered her fragile rib cage. Another followed it through the shattered bone and into her heart, rending the outer surface of her aorta. A third tore the aorta into mulch.

Blood gushing from her mouth even as her eyes widened in shock, Ms. Orange collapsed to the ground.

Walking up to her, forcing his vision not to swim, Bolan checked her vitals. Ms. Orange was no longer a threat to anyone. She was down and permanently out of play.

She was good. But the Executioner was better.

Assuming the Black Cross hadn't recruited anyone new—and Bolan was fairly certain they hadn't—there were only three assassins left to take care of. And one of them was down the hill at the safehouse.

Retrieving his Desert Eagle, Bolan took a couple of deep breaths with his eyes closed in the hopes that the concussion that Ms. Orange had given him would ease a bit.

Opening his eyes, he saw the terrain was still a bit wobbly.

He also felt heat on his side, and, looking over, he saw that the detonation of the C-4 had caused some of the branches to alight, and that fire had now spread to the leaves and one of the trees. It would be a full-fledged inferno before long.

But that didn't matter. Ms. White was incredibly dangerous, and Bolan wasn't sure that five marshals would be enough to keep Ami Pembleton alive.

Gripping the sleeve of Ms. Orange's shirt, he tore off two strips so he could use them as makeshift bandages for the wound on his arm. It took more time away from his pursuit of Ms. White, but he was woozy and he couldn't afford to add blood loss to the scenario.

Once the two strips were tied and knotted tightly around the wound, putting what he figured to be sufficient pressure on it to stop the bleeding, Bolan started running down the hill away from the fire.

**17**

Ami Pembleton was going stir-crazy.

"Look," she'd said when the federal marshals had taken her away to a safehouse, "this is a mistake."

"I'm afraid it isn't, ma'am," one of the marshals, whose name was Dalton, said in that annoying tone that law-enforcement types used when talking to civilians. Between being married to a Baltimore cop and working in Washington, D.C., Pembleton routinely encountered cops, Feds, marshals, Secret Service, and more, and they *all* talked like that—as if they were just humoring you by even talking to you while they did whatever the hell they wanted.

Just as she'd arrived at the B and B, she was met by the marshals who told her she must go with them right away. They then bunged her into a black SUV. The drive consisted of a bunch of twisty-turny roads that provided a lovely view of the local cow population.

When they'd arrived at this cottage in the middle of nowhere, another marshal—a woman named Guthrie— explained that someone was trying to kill her.

Pembleton had thought that to be the craziest thing she'd ever heard in her life.

She continued to believe that right up until the next day when she was watching the morning news discussing the explosion at the Johnson House Bed and Breakfast the previous night.

Running out of the bedroom, she went straight for Guthrie, who was sitting at a laptop in the living room. "What the hell happened? The B and B I was supposed to stay at has been blown up."

"We told you someone was trying to kill you, Ms. Pembleton," Guthrie had said. "And we made them think they succeeded."

Horrified, Pembleton had asked, "People think I'm *dead?*"

"Nobody's identified the remains yet—including the local PD—so the only ones who think you're dead are the people who are trying to kill you."

"Why is someone trying to kill me?"

"Do you have enemies, Ms. Pembleton?"

At that, she'd laughed. "The list would take an hour. But most of them—"

"Only takes *one* of them, ma'am," Guthrie had said.

Since watching that news report, Pembleton had understood the wisdom of her being hidden. She didn't like the fact that she couldn't call her husband, and she didn't like that she couldn't access the Internet in any way. But she also didn't like that someone was trying to kill her, and she didn't like not knowing *why* someone was trying to kill her. And either Guthrie and her fellow marshals didn't know or they couldn't tell her—one was as likely as the other— leaving her alone with her thoughts.

At least she'd brought a book to read on the train, but she had finished that while sitting around during the day.

Guthrie and Dalton were in the house with her, while three other marshals, whose names she never got, were patrolling outside.

Then she heard the explosion.

Immediately she ran to one of the barred windows.

Dalton came running in. "Get *away* from the windows, Ms. Pembleton!"

"Right, right," she said as she followed his instruction and sat on the end of the bed, which was in the center of the room. Apparently that was the safest place for her to be.

Outside, Marshals Anderson, Reagal and Travinsky all whirled at the telltale sound of one of the Claymores going off. They'd been told only that the woman inside needed to be protected and that the people going after her were resourceful. Each of them had been issued a 9 mm Beretta, which the agents pulled out as they raced to the hill side of the house.

Knowing that Guthrie and Dalton were taking care of securing the inside, Anderson pointed at Travinsky, then at the cistern next to the house.

The cistern was from before the place had its plumbing replaced and modernized, and Travinsky nodded and immediately took up position behind it, relative to the top of the hill. Anderson then pointed to his left, and Reagal fanned out that way, with Anderson himself going to the right.

All three held up their Berettas and waited for some sign of life.

The first sign came when a bullet whistled through the air over Anderson's head. Instinctively, he fired back, before he was even sure where the shot came from.

Even as he did so, more shots whistled through the air, and Anderson saw Reagal go down, blood splurting out the back of his head as a round tore through his skull. Bullets continued to fly, and finally Anderson saw his target: a woman in a navy blue jumpsuit running down the hill in a random pattern, dashing right and left haphazardly, shooting with a 9 mm OD Green Glock 19 in her right hand.

Her compact weapon was designed to be concealed, and was small enough that someone could fire it with one hand if necessary, and while running, especially if you weren't trying hard to hit anything specific. And she wasn't—this was just covering fire, and the shot on Reagal was a lucky one. Nothing else she fired had even come close.

Anderson took aim at where he expected her to run next.

Unfortunately, she outfoxed him and went another way, and by this time she was most of the way down the hill. Both of their advantages increased the closer she got, but there was one of her and four of them, so Anderson wasn't worried.

He shot again. This time the bullet winged her in the leg. She stumbled and fell to one knee, blood staining the now-ripped leg of the jumpsuit.

Then she held up her left hand and threw a Hibben knife right at Anderson.

She was still far enough away that Anderson was able to dive to the ground, but the knife caught him in the back of the leg, slicing through muscle and tendon and skin all the way to the other side of his shin, and embedding in the limestone driveway, pinning him to the ground.

Ignoring the pain that racked his entire leg, Anderson kept shooting at her—as did Travinsky from the safety of the cistern.

Then the woman reached into a pocket with her left hand and pulled out a grenade, yanking the firing pin with her teeth and throwing the bomb unerringly at the cistern.

"Travinsky!" Anderson cried even as Travinsky ran from the cistern.

But she wasn't fast enough. The grenade went off, the explosion's report ringing in Anderson's ears. The house itself was fine—it was armored against such a primitive attack—but no one had bothered to armor the cistern. The retreating Travinsky was pelted not only with shrapnel from the grenade, but also from the shattered concrete of the cistern. Her spinal cord was severed instantly in four different places from her neck to her hip, and she died immediately. Smoke billowed into the sky and away from the house, filling the air with an acrid stench.

Before Anderson could turn and fire on the woman again, he felt a bullet tear into his back. He tried to lift his arm to fire back but spots danced in front of his eyes even as the bullet that had collapsed his lung made breathing suddenly very difficult.

Two more bullets ended his last resistance to death.

Limping the rest of the way down the hill, Ms. White cursed Mr. Sapphire, whoever he really was. The Black Cross's background checks had never failed before, and Ms. White was furious at Mr. Indigo for his screwup on that front.

If she survived this, she was going to have some serious words with Mr. Indigo on that very subject.

She should have realized something was wrong when he insisted on hanging back while Mr. Blue set up his rifle. There was something about the way he looked, like he was expecting that Claymore to go off. He confirmed it after the Claymore *did* go off.

Having left him to the tender mercies of Ms. Orange, Ms. White continued with the job. If nothing else, Mr. Sapphire's betrayal and the death of Mr. Blue meant that Ms. White's share of this job would be much larger. Perhaps Mr. Sapphire would even take care of Ms. Orange, leaving Ms. White to kill the traitor herself and get the entire share.

And then she'd retire. She'd had enough of this. The risks were too great, and she was at the stage where she just wanted to find a tropical island to live on. Maybe seduce young men *without* killing them.

For now, though, she had a job to finish. She had taken out the three marshals guarding the house with ease, though she suffered a leg wound in the process. There were probably at least two still in the house, possibly more.

She had plenty more grenades, but the results of the first one proved that the next one would need to go off inside the house. The windows were barred, and probably wired, so her only real option was the front door. Stepping over the smoking remains of the cistern she'd destroyed, she moved slowly along the side of the house, staying under the windows. The people inside probably knew where she was, but there was no reason to make it easy for them.

Waiting two seconds, she then stuck her head and hands out around the corner, aiming her Glock at the front door.

There was no one there.

That made sense to Ms. White. Why come outside when the target was inside the safe, armored house?

Slowly, she approached the front door.

Then she saw movement on the other side of the house. Leaning against the wall, she waited to see what would happen.

The Executioner then showed his face and fired his Desert Eagle. Unfortunately, the concussion affected his aim, and the rounds whistled past Ms. White's face.

Her back still against the wall, Ms. White raised her left arm alongside the wall and fired the Glock. None of the shots hit Bolan, who had quickly retreated around the corner of the house. Most of them hit the house's aluminum siding or zoomed above where the Executioner's head had been and impacted on a nearby maple tree.

She kept firing until the Glock dry-clicked, and only then did she also take refuge around the corner of the house. The wind shifted, blowing the smoke from her destruction of the cistern toward her back, obscuring her view—but also obscuring her erstwhile comrade's.

While reloading the Glock, she said, "You were never one of us, were you, Mr. Sapphire? Who sent you to destroy us?"

No answer came. Spots broke out in front of Ms. White's eyes. At first she thought it to be the smoke, but then she looked down at her leg where the marshal had shot her. She had done nothing to bind the wound, not thinking it would take this long to take care of the other marshals—and Pembleton, if she was truly alive in there, which seemed likely.

Snapping the clip into place with a metallic click, Ms. White said, "Come now, Mr. Sapphire. One of us is about to die." Normally, she would have assumed in any given physical confrontation that her foe was the one about to die, but whoever Mr. Sapphire really was, he'd proved himself to be incredibly resilient, clever and dangerous. Just the fact that he had survived a direct confrontation with Ms. Orange was proof of that. Ms. White respected the killing skills of few people on this Earth aside from herself, but Ms. Orange, one of the original Black Cross, was one of them. "The least we deserve is truth between us."

Suddenly, she felt the cold metal of a muzzle pressed against her temple. "Damn," she said. "That was careless."

"You were the one who provided me with cover when you blew up the cistern," the Executioner said.

That and her wounded leg, but Ms. White wasn't about to say that. "Why are you doing this?" she asked instead. "A man with your skills would be of so much use to the Black Cross."

"Not for much longer. By this time tomorrow, the Black Cross will just be a bad memory."

"Again, I must ask, why? Did someone hire you?"

"That's *your* racket, Ms. White, not mine. You killed several government agents who should have been allowed to retire in peace."

"If you say so," Ms. White said. She almost shrugged but didn't want to risk any kind of sudden movement. "It was a job, I did it." She realized that she was dealing with a fanatic. She also noticed that he had lost the Southern accent. She suspected that Mr. Sapphire's past was entirely fabricated—though he obviously had *some* kind of military training.

"I do not suppose we could make a bargain," Ms. White said. "You intend to destroy the Black Cross. Very well—do so. I had intended to retire after this contract in any case. I have had my fill of this life. If it is your wish, you will never hear from me again. For that matter, if it is your wish, I can fulfill any of your most magnificent fantasies. I will do whatever you wish, Mr. Sapphire. Simply name it, and it is yours. All I ask in exchange is my life."

She turned her body slightly toward him, angling her body so that her breasts, which were practically spilling out of the jumpsuit, were obvious to him.

Bolan didn't even look down at what she was offering. "There's only one thing you have that I want."

"What is that?" she asked—and tried to wrest free to bring her weapon into play.

The Executioner squeezed the trigger of the Desert Eagle, blowing off her entire forehead. White collapsed to the muddy ground.

Answering her final question, the Executioner said, "Your life."

Stepping over her body, Bolan then went to the front door of the house and knocked on it, blinking his eyes a few times. His head injury was still affecting him, which was why he didn't actually take her out until he was right on top of her. Between the smoke and the concussion, he didn't trust himself to hit her the first time, and White was good enough that he *had* to get her with the first shot.

As he knocked, he said, "Clear!"

A few seconds later, Guthrie's face was in the window, and only then did she open the door, recognizing the Executioner's face. "Striker? Jesus, nobody told me *you* were in on this."

"Thought you were on the night shift, Guthrie."

"I was supposed to be, but my niece has a piano recital tonight that I promised I'd be there for—so I traded shifts with McSorley."

"I'm sorry about your people outside."

"Yeah, me, too."

"Is Ms. Pembleton all right?"

A voice sounded from behind Guthrie. "What the *hell* is going on?"

Looking past the marshal, Bolan saw the same face he'd been observing from a roof across from her house for a week. "Ms. Pembleton, some people want you dead enough to hire an elite group of assassins for the job. Don't worry, though, this will be the end of them."

"What is this about? Why are they trying to *kill* me?"

"Our best guess is it's about your attempts to investigate Fuster & Son."

"This is about the transport vehicle?" Pembleton looked both stunned and dismayed. "I do not *believe* this! Oh, Whelan's getting an *earful* next time I talk to him."

Leaving her to rant, Bolan looked at Guthrie. "Can you handle the cleanup, Guthrie?"

"Let me guess, you have to go off and blow more shit up?"

"Something like that. Do you have a first-aid kit?"

Guthrie stepped aside and led Bolan into the kitchen area. "Sure. Come on in. Dalton's already radioed the local fire department to take care of that blaze up the hill. Just do me a favor and get these guys, okay? This lady needs to get home safely, and Anderson, Travinsky and Reagal deserve the payback."

"That's the plan," Bolan said as Guthrie handed him a first-aid kit that had been stored under the kitchen table. Opening it, he found standard pressure bandages. Unknotting the makeshift bandage made from Ms. Orange's sleeve, he put on a pressure bandage.

"Er, you want a hand with that?" Guthrie asked, but by the time she finished the question, Bolan had already tied on the pressure bandage.

"Years of practice," he said. "Thanks for this. Now if you'll excuse me, I've got work to do."

He left and walked over to Ms. White's body. Rummaging in her pockets, he found her cell phone, as well as another of her Hibben knives. Working his way back up the hill—taking a slightly different route to avoid the fire—and trying to keep steady as he did so, he waited until he got to the tree line before pressing the number 5 and holding it.

Minutes later, he was at the clearing, fighting down nausea. As expected, the Black Hawk was waiting for him, along with Mr. Chartreuse and Mr. Silver. The engine was running, the rotors spinning, in anticipation of the need for a quick escape.

Upon seeing Bolan alone, Chartreuse hopped out of the Black Hawk. "What the hell happened?"

By way of answering, Bolan held up his SIG-Sauer and fired four times.

Chartreuse's body convulsed as the rounds pelted his chest, smashing his heart, lungs and stomach.

Mr. Silver immediately started lifting the Black

Hawk off the ground. Bolan ran for the chopper, taking a leap when he was ten feet away. Reaching out, his hands gripped the lip of the open entrance to the back compartment. Clambering up even as the Black Hawk lifted off, Bolan quickly ran to the front, whipping out the Hibben knife.

Still gripping the stick with one hand, Silver glanced behind himself and fired a .38 Smith & Wesson one-handed. Unfortunately, trying to fly the Black Hawk and shoot at the same time spoiled his shot, and the bullet flew harmlessly over Bolan's head and out the still-open entry. Wind started to whip through the aft compartment as the Black Hawk gained altitude.

Closing the gap between them in three quick steps, Bolan plunged the knife into the side of Silver's neck, the blood trickling down the side and onto his hand, but not on the windshield. Bolan's concussion-induced nausea was going to make flying the Black Hawk difficult enough, he didn't need visual obstructions on top of that.

The Black Hawk bucked and wove as Bolan threw Silver into the copilot's chair, then he got into the vacated seat and yoked the helicopter under his control. Gritting his teeth, Bolan forced the Black Hawk to straighten out and fly right.

Glancing at the fuel gauge, he saw that Silver had gassed up as promised. There was enough to get him to Chippewa County.

Bolan didn't have the sat phone handy, and even if he did, he didn't trust himself in his current condition to be able to hold a conversation with Brognola and fly the Black Hawk at the same time. Right now, he couldn't afford to take even one hand off the controls.

He just had to hope that, when Marshal Guthrie contacted her superiors, they would contact Brognola and fill him in.

There was still Mr. Indigo and the final two assassins to take care of. Bolan knew that Brognola had set in motion the arrest of Galloway so that he, at least, couldn't be used for further recruiting endeavors, but the Executioner still had to hope that the final, unknown assassins would be the end of it.

And before he took out Mr. Indigo, there were some questions the Executioner would need answered. Four good people who'd proudly served their country had died an ignominious death while enjoying what should have been a quiet retirement. Based on the last conversation Ms. White would ever have—and based on Bolan's own brief experiences with the Black Cross— the hired help weren't given explanations, only targets.

Before he died at the Executioner's hands, Bolan would extract the reason why from Mr. Indigo.

**18**

The Executioner had to focus all his concentration on gripping the stick of the UH-60L Black Hawk. His vision was swimming, and the landscape of Pennsylvania, Ohio and Michigan kept shifting and almost bouncing in his sights.

Several times, the radio sounded. At first, it was the young man at the laptop—whose nom de guerre Bolan had never learned. Then it was Mr. Indigo.

Bolan ignored the calls. For one thing, if he took both hands off the stick in his current state, he risked crashing the Black Hawk. For another, he had nothing to say to them. It was better for them to live in ignorance, and be surprised by Bolan's arrival at the Chippewa County headquarters.

By the time he found himself approaching the headquarters, Mr. Indigo's voice over the radio sounded incredibly strained.

"Mr. Silver!" the head of the Black Cross said. "Mr. Chartreuse! Somebody answer, dammit!"

The Black Hawk bucked and wove as Bolan tried desperately to lower it as best he could, but it felt as if someone was stirring his brain matter with a spoon.

With a bone-jarring thud, the Black Hawk hit the ground, rattling Bolan in his seat.

He shut down the Black Hawk and pulled out the last bit of C-4 he had left after blowing up the Johnson House, as well as a cell-phone detonator, and placed it in the lap of the late Mr. Silver.

The young man at the laptop came out of the cabin, running toward the Black Hawk.

"Jesus, Sapphire, is that you? What the hell happened? Indigo's about ready to have a *cow,* he—"

Forcing himself to remain steady, Bolan clipped his cell phone to his belt, leaving it open, and having already typed in the ten digits that would, when he hit Talk, ring the cell phone on the C-4. Then he stepped out of the Black Hawk, pointing his SIG-Sauer right at the young man's head.

"Take me inside."

"Jesus! What the *hell,* dude?" The young man threw up his hands, completely not expecting this turn of events. "Where's Chartreuse and Silver?"

"As dead as you'll be if you don't take me inside to where Indigo is."

"Okay, okay!" He turned around slowly and started walking toward the HQ.

"Slow down," Bolan said. He needed to take measured paces if he wasn't going to let the concussion get the best of him, so he gave that instruction to the young man, who obliged by taking shorter paces.

The Executioner then asked, "Who else is inside?"

"Just Indigo and Black and Gray."

"Both Black and Gray, huh?" Bolan assumed these to be the two final assassins.

"Dude, what happened to your accent?"

"Shut up and keep walking."

"That's as far as you go, Mr. Sapphire," said a voice from behind Bolan. The person spoke with a thick South American accent.

Cursing himself for the concussion, Bolan glanced out of the corner of his eye to see a tall, lanky Latino man carrying a Heckler & Koch USP pistol, pointed at Bolan's head.

Normally, this man—whom the Executioner assumed to be one of the final two assassins in the Black Cross's current employ—would never have gotten the drop on Bolan, but he was not in a normal state at the moment. He sneaked up on Bolan as easily as the Executioner had snuck up on Ms. White. It was taking all of Bolan's focus to keep the SIG-Sauer steady in his hands and pointed at the young man while moving slowly forward.

"You Mr. Black or Mr. Gray?" Bolan asked.

The man smiled, revealing a gold tooth. "No shades of gray with me, Sapphire—I'm Mr. Black, and you're a dead man."

"I don't think so. If you don't allow me to keep going inside, I will shoot this man."

"What, this man?" Black whirled and shot the young man in the back. The 9 mm rounds plowed into the boy's spine, severing it in an instant. He was dead before his face impacted with the ground.

The time Black took to take that shot was enough time for Bolan to whirl and aim his SIG-Sauer at him, but not enough time to shoot before the muzzle of the H&K was facing Bolan's own concussed head.

"He's replaceable. There are a million kids like him in the world, bunch of geeks all desperate for money so they can feed their video game addiction. We can find fifty more like him in an hour."

"No, you won't," Bolan said.

"Why is that?"

"Because the Black Cross comes to an end this day. When the Black Cross hired Mr. Sapphire, it put their fighting strength at seven. Mr. Pink, Mr. Blue, Ms. Orange, and Ms. White are all dead. So, by the way, are Mr. Chartreuse and Mr. Silver, and you just killed the last member of the support team. That just leaves you and one more assassin—and Mr. Indigo. I intend to kill the three of you now."

Black laughed heartily but he never took his eyes off Bolan. "Are you serious? The Black Cross has endured for several decades. What makes you think *you* can stop it?"

"Experience."

"I don't know who you really are, Sapphire, but do you know who I am?"

"No," the Executioner said. "I don't much care."

"Yeah? Well, I don't much care who you are, either, but I can tell you this. I was born and raised in Chile. I was just a boy when Pinochet took over in '73. I learned how to shoot a gun before I could grow a mustache. I killed my first man before I slept with my first woman, and I lost track of the number of people I've killed since then."

Bolan still didn't care, but as long as Black was talking, he wasn't shooting, and the Executioner was just waiting for his best opportunity to hit the Talk button on the cell phone attached to his belt. He just needed the right moment, but the longer Black babbled, the more likely it was that moment would come.

Black was still going on. "But then Pinochet got weak, so I went elsewhere. I went to the desert and worked for the oil barons. They pay nice in the desert if you kill people for them and protect their oil. Worked for Khaddafi, worked for Saddam. I spent my whole life killing people, and I'm better at it than anyone alive. You know how I know this? I've already killed anyone who might be better at it."

"Really?" Bolan didn't have to work very hard to sound unimpressed, as bravado had never been high on the list of things that made an impression on the Executioner.

"You don't believe me?" Black stared at Bolan with hard eyes. "You think I'm lying?"

"Honestly? I didn't care before you started talking, and I care less now. My only interest is in seeing the Black Cross destroyed."

"It will never happen. As long as I am Black Cross, the Black Cross will endure. Because nobody can kill me, you hear? *Nobody!* I'm *muerte*—the embodiment of death! I survived Pinochet, Khaddafi, Saddam and *all* those people! You think after all that, that I'm afraid of *you?*"

"Again," Bolan said, relaxing his body as if to indicate that he was bored, which included letting one arm fall to his side, "I don't really care that much."

Black sneered and shook his head. "You're pathetic, you know that? You think you can fire that peashooter at me with one hand? Go ahead, take a shot one-handed! This ought to be hilarious!"

To the Executioner's astonishment, Black actually lowered his H&K.

Bolan's finger immediately went to the Talk button on his cell phone.

Braced and ready for the explosion, Bolan, even concussed as he was, was able to keep his footing on the dirt as the C-4 detonated, destroying the Black Hawk in a cacophonous, fiery conflagration.

Black wasn't so fortunate, and the concussive blast of the Black Hawk, even though he was a good forty feet away from it, sent him falling forward.

Gripping the SIG-Sauer with both hands, Bolan squeezed off eight rounds. Four bullets penetrated Black's spine, three more went through his side and the last went in his neck.

The fire from the exploding Black Hawk sent heat cascading onto Bolan's face. He knew that there was still another assassin, plus Indigo, to deal with.

A bullet whizzed by Bolan's head, and he immediately fell to the ground.

That action caused his head to swim, and nausea to rise to the fore. Two more bullets whizzed by, originating, he realized, from above. Looking up, he tried to figure out where it was coming from.

Unfortunately, the smoke from the burning Black Hawk was drifting upward, just as that of the destroyed cistern had in Brady's Bend, making visibility difficult. Now as then, it worked in Bolan's favor, since the smoke obscured the vision of the sniper—likely the final assassin—and heat-sensitive sights wouldn't be of much use with the fire raging.

ON THE ROOF of the HQ, Mr. Gray peered through the sights of his 5.56 mm Smith & Wesson M&P15T rifle and cursed Mr. Sapphire for gumming up the works with that explosion. His visibility was shot to hell.

If he had gotten to the roof a few minutes sooner, there wouldn't have been a problem, but he'd used up precious time trying to figure out what was going on. Their tech guy—Mr. Gray had never bothered to learn the young man's name—had been sent out by Mr. Indigo to meet the Black Hawk and find out what the hell had happened. When he didn't come back in anything resembling the time it would take to fetch someone, Mr. Indigo looked out the window, only to see that Mr. Black and Mr. Sapphire were facing off, there was no sign of Ms. White, Ms. Orange, Mr. Blue, Mr. Silver or Mr. Chartreuse, and the tech guy was lying dead on the ground in a pool of muddy blood.

Just as Mr. Gray had gotten to the roof, he saw Mr. Sapphire touch something on his belt, and then the Black Hawk blew up. Mr. Gray set up his S&W rifle in record time, but by then Mr. Sapphire had put almost a dozen bullets into Mr. Black.

Mr. Gray had no objection to seeing Mr. Black lying dead on the ground, as Mr. Gray had always found the man to be an arrogant twit. He was constantly going on about who he worked for in his time. But he was good at killing people, which was why the Black Cross kept him around.

Before joining the Black Cross, Mr. Gray was named Erick Lagdanen, and he had been a Navy SEAL. He'd been a sniper and had worked his way up to Master Chief before Commander Simone finally drove him to the breaking point.

For years, people had been telling Lagdanen that he

needed to go to Officer Candidate School, that he'd make a better officer than most of his peers. But Lagdanen never bothered to fill out the application for OCS, even though officers kept giving copies to him, because he knew he'd hate it. Yeah, the pay would be better, but he had yet to meet an officer who'd earned his respect. Why become one of the people who he felt the urge to punch in the nose every single day?

When he'd been put under Simone's command, he finally gave into that urge. Simone suffered a broken nose and Lagdanen suffered a dishonorable discharge and time in Leavenworth.

When he got out, he had very few options, as the only skills he had were ones given to him by his Navy training. Unfortunately, his criminal record precluded any jobs in law enforcement, and that left him with few job prospects beyond that of menial labor, which he refused to do.

Luckily, some old Navy buddies, who'd been equally disenchanted with the state of the U.S. Navy had need of his services. After all, there were organizations other than the armed forces and law enforcement who needed people to be shot through a rifle's sights.

Eventually, he found his way into the employ of the Black Cross. One of the jobs he'd done had gotten the attention of that organization because Lagdanen's target had also been theirs—only Lagdanen beat them to it, costing the Black Cross most of its fee. Mr. Indigo had tracked down Lagdanen and brought him to the Black Cross's headquarters—at the time, just outside Kayenta, Arizona—telling Lagdanen that Indigo had two options before him: kill Lagdanen, or offer him a job.

To Lagdanen's relief, he went with the latter option.

He became Mr. Gray, and made a lot more money than he had as a mercenary or than he would have had he gone to OCS.

He'd just gotten back from a solo job—a rich man who wanted his mistress eliminated rather than risk his wife learning of her existence, which really didn't require an entire team—and was then told by Mr. Indigo of the Black Cross's other job having gone rather badly, including the death of Mr. Pink. With that, the death of Mr. Black, the other losses they'd taken after the retired spooks gig and the possible other deaths indicated by Mr. Sapphire arriving solo, Mr. Gray was thinking that a lot of new recruiting would be happening.

Peering into his reticle, he was able to make out a vague shape on the ground, and he shot at it.

BOLAN WINCED IN PAIN as another bullet whizzed through the air, slicing into his left arm, just above the wound that had been made by the Claymore. The bullet went all the way through, burying itself in the dirt beneath the Executioner, but the white-hot agony that sizzled through his arm indicated that the limb would be all but useless until he got it treated properly.

But he couldn't afford to let that happen. Grinding his teeth to plow through the pain, he forced his left arm to move so he could solidly grip the SIG-Sauer with both hands.

The wind shifted, and the smoke blew in another direction, so for an instant, Bolan had a clear shot. But since Gray had the same good shot, the Executioner had to make it count.

Squeezing the trigger, his first shot hit the barrel of

the rifle, deflecting it upward and ruining Gray's shot. The sniper then overcompensated, bringing the rifle down at a lower angle toward the ground.

Ignoring the pain that was burning his left arm, Bolan fired off his last three rounds.

One shot flew over Gray's head. The third winged him in the arm. But that didn't matter so much, as the second shot hit right at the reticle. Shattering the glass on one end, it shot through the sight to the other end, shattering the lenses and destroying the electronics inside, before breaking through to the other side and lodging in Gray's right eye.

Traveling through the reticle did enough to retard the 9 mm round's velocity that the bullet didn't penetrate all the way through to the brain, but Gray's right eye was completely pulped by the bullet. The pain was beyond agony, and Gray—who was a man used to pain, having gone through SEALs training—rolled onto his side, his rifle abandoned, writhing in the agony that accompanied a lead slug lodged in a most sensitive body part.

Bolan heard the man's screams and knew that it was safe to get to his feet. Mr. Gray wouldn't be shooting anybody anytime soon.

As soon as he rose to stand upright, the entire world swam and shook. The Executioner closed his eyes and mentally forced himself to stop suffering the effects of the concussion. It didn't entirely work, but it was successful enough to keep him steady on his feet as he stepped over the corpses of Mr. Black and the young man and headed into the headquarters.

Mr. Gray was no longer a factor. That just left Mr. Indigo.

**19**

Bolan ejected the empty magazine from his SIG-Sauer and rammed home a fresh one. He did likewise for the Desert Eagle, even though he hadn't gone through the entire clip yet. He preferred to have them full, just in case there were more surprises inside. Then he ripped off a piece of the bloody shirt worn by the young man and used it as a tourniquet for the wound in his left arm. The agony was almost unbearable, but he couldn't afford any more blood loss. That arm was going to be difficult enough to use as it was.

Slowly, careful not to strain his concussed head any more than he absolutely had to, Bolan moved toward the cabin HQ, his SIG-Sauer at the ready, with the Desert Eagle available as backup.

The Executioner was encouraged by the lack of a response from anyone as he approached the building. He stood to the left of the front door and threw it open, SIG-Sauer held high—but no one was on the other side. There was just an empty hallway.

Slowly, Bolan worked his way down that hall, past a staircase, to a large room at the back of the cabin. He could hear the hum of equipment.

As soon as he entered, he saw the bald head and lanky form of Indigo, sitting at a laptop. Bolan couldn't make out what was on the screen—his vision was getting progressively more impaired by his concussion—but he suspected that Indigo was doing whatever purging procedure preceded a move to a new location.

Without preamble, Bolan said, "Put your hands behind your head, fingers interlocked. *Now!* If you *touch* that keyboard, I will shoot you in the head."

Indigo hesitated, then did as he was told. "I should've realized it was you, Burns," he said as he interlaced his fingers behind his smooth head. "You were just too good to be true. But Galloway doesn't usually give me bad recruits. I suppose you set up Mr. Pink."

"Actually, no," the Executioner said. "He really did try to run me off the road. Saved me the trouble of hunting him down and killing him the way I did the rest of your people."

"Really?" Indigo sounded remarkably calm.

"Really. White, Orange, Blue, Chartreuse, Silver, Black, Gray—all the members of your little rainbow coalition of assassins are dead. So's the man who used to sit at that laptop. You're the only one left. The Black Cross is defeated."

"I have to admit, I'm impressed. Your service record didn't indicate anywhere near that level of skill."

"Whether or not you're impressed is of little interest to me. What I want to know is: Who hired you to kill Albert Bethke, Michaela Grosso, Terrence Redmond and Richard Lang? And who hired you to kill Ami Pembleton?"

Indigo was still facing away from Bolan, but the Executioner could hear the incredulousness in his voice. "*That's* what this is about?"

"You killed four people who'd served their country with distinction and should have been permitted to enjoy their retirement, and you tried to kill an innocent woman. Destroying your entire organization is the very *least* that you all deserve. You're going to tell me who hired you. No matter what happens."

"What possible reason would I have for telling you that? You've killed all my assassins, and my support staff. You're obviously going to kill me next. If I tell you what you want to know, I've lost the only leverage I have to keep myself alive. And don't expect to find it on this laptop, either—I've purged it, down to the operating system. Right now, this thing's a glorified paperweight."

Bolan then shot Indigo in the left calf.

Indigo screamed as the bullet sliced through muscle and bone, pulverizing the former and shattering the latter. He fell to the floor, his hands no longer interlaced as his hands instinctively went to his destroyed limb. "Son of a *bitch!*"

Then Bolan shot Indigo's right calf in roughly the same spot.

"You're now crippled for life, and suffering extreme pain," Bolan said, though Indigo's screams indicated that he was well aware of the second part, at least. "If you don't tell me who hired you to kill Bethke, Grosso, Redmond and Lang, and who hired you to kill Pembleton, I'll shoot both your arms. I won't kill you. Instead, you'll be a paraplegic and spend the rest of your life in extreme pain, no matter how many painkillers you ingest."

Tears were streaming down Indigo's cheeks. This wasn't the first time he'd been shot. When he was a uniform in the LAPD, James Moreland was wounded in the line of duty while trying to subdue a member of the Crips gang who was high on crystal meth and was convinced that Officer Moreland and his partner were woolly mammoths stampeding in his crib. Moreland took a 9 mm round to his side; he still had the scar.

At the time, he had thought it to be the worst pain he'd ever feel in his life. It was as if someone had stuck a red-hot knife in his belly and left it there. The pain didn't go away until they put him under in the ER. After he woke up, the pain lingered, no matter how much morphine they dripped into his bloodstream.

That pain was nothing compared to what Mr. Indigo felt now. Shards of bone cut up through his skin and into his muscles.

But Indigo was not about to give in to this man who had destroyed everything he'd spent years caretaking.

And it was then that a voice in the back of his head said, *Caretaking what, exactly? A bunch of murderers?*

Almost as if he wanted to hear the right answer, Indigo looked up at Sapphire or Michael Burns or whatever the hell his real name was, and asked, "What's it to you? Why do you care who hired us for those two jobs?"

"I already told you," the Executioner said. "They served their country and had earned quiet retirements. You took that from them, but you took your orders from someone else. As for Pembleton, I'm fairly certain I know who it was who ordered the hit on her—I just want you to confirm it."

Bolan hoped that he could convince Indigo soon, because he was quickly losing his ability to see straight. Right now the image of Indigo in front of him was hazy and indistinct, and kept threatening to split in two. If he started getting double vision, he had no way to be sure that he would be shooting the right one.

Indigo wasn't thinking about answering Bolan's question, though. He was thinking about an oath he took to serve and protect the people of the City of Los Angeles. He had believed in that once, but let that belief fall by the wayside because his superiors were jackasses. They were interested in statistics, in the appearance of fighting crime, but mostly in making sure they looked good to the public. The actual work of fighting crime was something they frowned on, as it was something that cost money and effort. LaMont Hawkins, the future Mr. Pink, had committed murder on a scale that made John Wayne Gacy look like a piker, and the LAPD brass didn't even believe he existed. How could he have continued to work for people with their heads that far up their own asses?

But had that been a good enough reason to go back on his oath? Worse, to facilitate murder in excess of anything he saw in a decade in Robbery-Homicide?

What had he turned into?

Before he could say anything, several shots rang out in the cabin.

Bolan felt a steel-jacketed bullet carve into his right shoulder blade and shoot out the other side. Gathering up every inch of willpower, he kept himself from falling over. His shoulder felt as if it were on fire, but the shot hadn't appeared to hit any bones or major arteries. The Executioner knew that was just dumb luck.

Then again, maybe it was good luck, since five shots rang out in the cabin and that was the only one that hit anything.

Turning around slowly in deference to his concussion, he saw that Mr. Gray wasn't out of commission quite yet.

Blood and optic fluid oozed out of the remains of his right eye socket as he stumbled into the room. He was holding a Glock in his hands and squeezing off rounds seemingly at random.

"You fucking son of a bitch!" Gray roared in a slurred voice. "I'll kill you!"

The Executioner took a moment to aim his SIG-Sauer. Unfortunately, that moment gave Gray enough time to hide behind one of the desks in the room.

Bolan went ahead and let loose several shots anyhow, but the 9 mm rounds from his pistol just richocheted off the metal desk.

Gray held up his Glock and fired wildly.

The Executioner closed his eyes tight, forced himself to focus. He didn't bother taking cover—the way Gray was randomly firing, he was just as safe where he was standing as he would be anywhere else, so he might as well stay put and get a good shot off.

He opened his eyes and fired six shots under the desk.

Five shots ricocheted as the first one had, but one went under and hit Gray in the leg. Screaming, Gray held up his Glock and continued to fire, but most of his shots were now flying into the ceiling.

Slowly, Bolan walked to the desk. "It's over," he said as he kept his SIG-Sauer pointed at what was left of Gray's face.

"Go to hell," Gray said, raising his Glock and pointing it right at Bolan.

"You first." Bolan squeezed the trigger. The 9 mm round sizzled through the air and penetrated Gray's forehead. With nothing to slow it down, the bullet had no difficulty cutting through skin, skull and brain matter. The power of the SIG-Sauer's firing chamber was enough to blow out the entire back of Gray's head, sending blood, bone fragments and gray matter splattering on the floor beneath him.

Slowly, Bolan turned around and looked at Indigo.

"I'm impressed," Indigo said through gritted teeth. "You've been shot at least twice, you've obviously got a concussion, and you're still what we used to call the baddest mother on the block."

"Nobody talks like that anymore," Bolan said, keeping his gun on the man.

Indigo looked at Bolan through tearstained eyes. "I used to be a cop, ya know."

Bolan neither knew nor cared, but he assumed if Indigo was going all confessional on him that perhaps there would be an answer to the Executioner's questions at the end of the litany.

So he prompted, "Why'd you quit?"

"Got tired of the bullshit. Too many people trying to cover their asses and play political games, and not enough who actually wanted to stop the bad guys."

"So you became a bad guy?"

"That wasn't how I looked at it. I'd spent all my time on the job getting played. So I thought I'd play back."

"And you never thought about who you were killing?"

"Never *cared*." Indigo winced and let out a long groan. The pain was obviously getting to him, but he was doing everything he could to keep it from showing. In an odd sort of way, Bolan admired that.

Indigo continued, "I just thought that nobody else gave a damn, so why should I? I didn't even think about who was being killed. I figured if somebody wanted to pay that much to get someone dead, they probably had good reason. Or at least they thought they did."

"Who thought that Bethke, Grosso, Redmond and Lang deserved to die?"

"Name's Robertson. Master Sergeant Timothy Robertson, United States Army Special Forces."

Bolan's eyes grew wide. "Excuse me?"

"You heard me."

"You're lying."

"Yeah, 'cause sitting here in agony's my idea of a good time. I'm tired of it, Sapphire. I want you to just take that Desert Eagle and make me eat it. I'm telling you right now, Sergeant Robertson is the one who hired us to kill those four. If you wanna know why, ask him. He didn't tell, and I didn't ask."

Bolan gritted his teeth. He'd look into Robertson when he got back to the Farm. "I assume that someone at Fuster went after Pembleton?"

"They bankrolled it, but the hit was ordered by someone in the NSA named Bradlee. Fuster paid for his summer home, so that's not exactly a big shock." Indigo smiled grimly. "Remember what I said before about bullshit?"

"All right then." Bolan holstered the SIG-Sauer.

"Good hunting," Indigo said.

"Thanks." Bolan hesitated. "What was your name before?"

"Detective James Moreland, LAPD Robbery-Homicide Unit."

Nodding, the Executioner said, "Well, Detective, it's time to make amends."

Bolan called Stony Man Farm to have the man picked up. He'd let his fellow cops deal with him now.

**20**

"Striker, you need medical attention."

With fresh bandages on his right shoulder and left arm, and having swallowed plenty of analgesics, Bolan didn't agree with Brognola's assessment—at least not yet. There was still work to be done, after all.

"Do you have the information I asked for?" Bolan queried, having just entered the War Room at Stony Man.

With a heavy sigh, Brognola tapped the track pad on the laptop on the conference room table. The large screen on the wall that it was plugged into lit up with a U.S. Army dossier for Master Sergeant Timothy Robertson. Currently inactive after doing three tours in Afghanistan.

Peering at the dates on the screen, Bolan said, "His last tour ended about a month before Bethke, Redmond, Grosso and Lang were killed. The question is, why would he want them dead?"

"Kurtzman actually dug up the connection," Brognola said, opening another window. "Thirty years ago, there was a covert op in the Soviet Union to retrieve a defector. They got him out, but one soldier was captured and sent to a gulag, where he was tortured by the KGB until he died of an infection. Note the soldier's name."

Again peering at the screen, the Executioner saw that one Corporal Saul Robertson did not make it home, and was later reported killed. His body was eventually sent home after the Soviet Union fell.

"Okay," Bolan said, "so his father was killed during an op."

Pointing at the memo that led off the file on the screen, Brognola said, "Look at the CC list. Grosso was the CIA's field agent for the op, with Lang as her supervisor back at Langley. Bethke was the NSA liaison with the CIA and the Army, and Redmond was the one who first communicated with the defector and set the plan in motion."

Letting out a long breath, Bolan sat back in the conference room chair. "So that explains it. Robertson blamed those four for his father's imprisonment and death."

"And torture."

"You have a line on Robertson?"

Brognola nodded. "But you should wait—"

"No," Bolan interrupted. "Robertson's even more responsible than the Black Cross. The assassins were just doing what they were paid to do, and that was worth me hunting them down. This man was a *soldier,* and he still took it upon himself to assassinate four good people. He has to pay for that. And so does Bradlee."

With a heavy sigh, Brognola said, "Fine." He handed Bolan a memory stick. "Everything Bear could find out about Robertson is on this. He's living in Paola, Kansas."

"Good. I'll take care of Bradlee, then Robertson."

"I still think you should get medical attention first."

"I've gotten all the medical attention I need," the

Executioner said as he got to his feet and pocketed the memory stick. "I don't have time to rest."

With that, he left.

ALLEN BRADLEE FINISHED his Reuben sandwich while reading the letters-to-the-editor section of the *Washington Post.* Downing the last of his root beer, he folded up the paper and went to his car.

While he presented an outward calm, he was incredibly frantic. Sometimes that calm facade cracked, as he'd yelled at Glynis twice that afternoon for things that weren't her fault, something he never did in the normal course of things.

But Ami Pembleton was still alive, and repeated calls to Higby's Imports and Exports went unanswered.

Sadly, Bradlee could not do likewise for the calls from General Spencer, who kept calling every day asking why the hell their problem hadn't been taken care of. This morning's call was the worst. "Now it looks like the bitch has gotten Whelan on her side. What in Christ's name is taking these people so goddamn long, Allen? It's your mess—fix it!"

Every call ended with those words. Bradlee wasn't sure exactly how the mess got to be his exclusive property— though he freely admitted that he had done the most to facilitate Fuster's "favored-nation" status with the DOD.

Bradlee walked to his car and pushed the button on his keychain that unlocked it. Tossing the *Post* onto the passenger seat, he climbed in and started the ignition. He barely paid attention to what he was doing, so it wasn't until he looked in the rearview mirror that he realized someone was sitting in the back seat.

It was no easy task to jump straight up in the air while sitting in a bucket seat while strapped in by a seat belt, but Bradlee managed it.

"Keep driving," the Executioner said from the back seat. His SIG-Sauer was pointed at Bradlee's head. "If you show any indication that anything's untoward, I will blow your head off."

"Who are you?"

"That doesn't matter. What matters is who *you* are, Allen Bradlee. Keep driving, I said."

His hands now shaking, Bradlee turned right out of the deli's driveway and headed toward the Baltimore-Washington Parkway, which would take him back to Fort Meade.

Assuming he lived that long.

Bolan kept talking. "You are a person who was given oversight over the choosing of a contractor to make a troop carrier. This was supposed to be a vehicle that would protect our soldiers in the field of battle. Instead of letting the best contractor take the job, you manipulated events so that Fuster & Son would get the contract. That was ten years ago, Mr. Bradlee, and the transporter still doesn't exist. You've endangered our troops. And if that was all you had done, it would be fine. You're just a bureaucrat, after all, and sometimes things like that happen when bureaucrats do their jobs."

Bradlee merged into traffic on the BWP, hoping that the fact that he was driving in fast-moving traffic—well, as fast as traffic ever moved on the BWP, anyhow—meant that he wouldn't be shot in the head.

Bolan went on, "But then you hired the Black Cross."

At that, Bradlee almost drove off the road. "Who *are* you?" he asked in a cracked voice.

"I told you that doesn't matter. What does matter is that you hired assassins to kill an innocent woman, who's only trying to get at the truth. And that is something that cannot be forgiven. Your position and your friends in the Pentagon protect you from the law—but nothing will protect you from justice. Get off the highway," Bolan said as they were approaching the exit for NSA headquarters.

"Who the hell *are* you?" Bradlee repeated.

"Drive to your parking spot," Bolan simply said.

Bradlee did so, pulling the car into his assigned space.

"Look, it wasn't just me, all right? General Spencer was the one who told me to—"

As he spoke, Bradlee started turning toward Bolan. As he discreetly reached for something between the seats, Bolan saw the silver glint of a gun. The executioner swiftly fired a 9 mm round into the side of Bradlee's head.

As Bradlee's body slumped forward, the Executioner departed through the backseat door, one more part of his mission complete.

BOLAN PEERED through the Pentax Lightseeker XL scope on his .50-caliber ArmaLite AR-50 BMG precision rifle. He sat on the roof of an apartment building in Paola, Kansas, that was across the street from a small house that was owned by Master Sergeant Timothy Robertson.

This was the Executioner's third day on this rooftop. Every time he'd had Robertson in his sights, either Robertson's wife or one of his two children were also present. While Bolan regretted the need to make Mrs. Robertson a widow and her son and daughter fatherless, it needed to be done—but he would not force them to see Robertson die. They were not complicit in his crime.

Bolan had seen his own family destroyed by the Mafia. Under no circumstances would he subject anyone else to that.

Which meant he had to be patient.

His words to Brognola notwithstanding, he was not in the best shape of his life. The aspirin only did so much for the concussion and the pain of his two wounds, but anything stronger would impair his ability to function, and Bolan simply could not allow that.

The one advantage to having to wait until Robertson was alone was that, as each day went by, he got better. Time truly did heal all wounds, and with each day that passed, his vision swam less, the pain in his arms lessened, and the functionality of those arms increased.

After the Robertson family went to bed on the night of the third day, Bolan packed up his rifle and went back to the motel where he'd been staying.

Staring at the stucco ceiling in the motel, unable to sleep, Bolan thought about Robertson and what had to have driven him to do what he had. In his record, Bolan saw a man very much like himself: a dedicated soldier and an ideal Special Forces candidate from the first day of training, who served with distinction on all three tours he took in the desert.

Obviously, at some point during that third tour, he found out about what actually happened to his father.

Bolan knew why the Black Cross assassins did what they did: they were paid. He knew why Allen Bradlee hired the assassins to kill Ami Pembleton: he, too, was paid. The paper trail Bear had found connecting Bradlee to Fuster & Son was appalling. That information had made its way in an anonymous e-mail to Ami Pembleton, and would surely be used as ammunition in her crusade to get Congress to investigate the contract.

But Bolan didn't know why a man with a wife and children and a mortgage felt the need to hire the Black Cross—whose services did not come cheap—to kill four people who had done nothing to deserve such retribution. Yes, they were involved in the mission that led to his father's death, but the elder Robertson knew the risks when he signed up.

And so did his son, who, after all, swore the same oath his father had.

So on the fourth day, Bolan got into the Toyota Camry he had rented and followed Robertson to his place of employment: a consulting firm in Kansas City. Originally, Bolan hadn't scoped out Robertson's workplace, since that was a bit too crowded.

But first, he wanted to talk.

It was a pleasant day outside, and Robertson took his lunch break around 1:00 p.m., getting lunch from a food court near his office and then sitting on a bench in a park.

Robertson had the bench to himself, so Bolan moved to it and sat next to him. Robertson glared at him when he did so, especially since there were other unoccupied benches.

"I know who you are, Sergeant," Bolan said. "More to the point, I know what you've done."

"What the hell're you—"

"I know you hired the Black Cross to kill Albert

Bethke, Michaela Grosso, Terrence Redmond and Richard Lang."

Robertson said nothing.

"Terrence Redmond was a friend of mine. And all four of them were good people who served their country—just like you did, and just like your father did."

Snarling, Robertson said, "You don't know a thing about my father."

"Corporal Saul Robertson, U.S. Army Special Forces, captured by Soviet forces during Operation Tunnel Vision thirty years ago, died in custody. And I'm fully aware of the role those four people played in that op."

"If you know all this, then why the hell do you even have to ask why I hired the Black Cross?"

"Because your father signed up for a dangerous job, and he knew the risks of getting caught. He was prepared for it—just as you were when you got your SF training."

"You don't understand."

"I was Army Special Forces, Sergeant. And I've never stopped fighting. I know the risks, and I know what's at stake. And I also know that there are good people doing the best they can in a dangerous world. Four of those people are dead now because you decided to blow your kids' college fund on killing them."

"It was an inheritance."

Bolan frowned. "Excuse me?"

"My grandfather had a ton of cash he never told anyone about. With Dad dead, it went to me when he died three years ago. My Army pension'll cover most of the kids' college. This money wasn't expected or planned for, and it was just enough to make those four bastards pay for what they did to my dad. And I'd do it again, if I need to."

Robertson's voice was laced with anger and resentment, and not a bit of repentance. Four good people were dead, and their murderer wasn't in the least bit sorry. Even Indigo—or, rather, Detective Moreland—came around in the end.

"They didn't do anything to your father," Bolan said. "The KGB did."

"We can do this dance all day, pal. What is it you want?"

"I wanted to know why."

"Well, now you do. So what happens next?"

Bolan stood up. "I suggest sending your wife and kids away tonight."

With that, the Executioner turned and walked away. He returned to his rental car and drove back to Paola to set up on the roof.

Regardless of who was home this night, Timothy Robertson would die before the sun came up. And if he tried to run away, the Executioner would find him.

Then, the mission would finally be over.

Until the next one.